GEORGE WASHINGTON
AT WAR—1776

John Koopman III

GEORGE WASHINGTON AT WAR—1776

JOHN KOOPMAN III

Library of Congress Cataloging-in-Publication Data
Koopman, John III
George Washington at War—1776 / John Koopman III
p. cm.
Includes bibliographic references.

Printed in the United States of America

Book design by Maureen Cutajar
www.gopublished.com

Cover: Painting by Don Troiani
www.historicalimagebank.com

Illustrations by Sariah Clonts

ISBN-13: 978-1514287781
ISBN-10: 1514287781

To the soldiers of the Continental Army of the American War of Independence, who fought for the freedom we enjoy today.

CONTENTS

Foreword

THE AMERICAN WAR of Independence as a fast-paced action novel? George Washington starring as an 18th-century Sylvester Stallone in a wild horse chase with the predictable outcome of our hero getting away, saved by rescuers appearing seemingly out of nowhere? Historical fiction as history worth reading?

Many history aficionados will turn away, shuddering in dismay at the thought, sensing that another magnum opus has appeared on the market that is probably not worth the paper it was printed on. Frequently their gut feeling is correct, but every so often there is a volume that shows that historical fiction can be good history and very much worth the time spent reading it.

John Koopman's *George Washington at War—1776* is one of these rare products that mixes sound, thoroughly researched history into historical fiction to provide the human facets of the American War of Independence that all too often get lost in traditional accounts of that conflict. Using primary sources such as pension applications by participants to tell his story, Koopman shows us that war involves killing and getting killed, that it is a bloody mess that knows no "nice" way of killing the enemy. Focusing on a few events in 1776, he also shows us the humane and the human side of that war, the compassion for the defeated enemy and the burden of command.

And yes, *George Washington at War—1776* does on occasion also read like an action novel. Only an expert horseman—and long-time Washington impersonator—such as Koopman could tell the story in which we anxiously accompany the commander-in-chief on his daring escape from a detachment of the 17th Light Dragoons. Koopman's first venture into historical fiction is not a complete and thorough history of the Boston and New York campaigns. It is meant to be fact-based historical fiction, and as such it is a great read and educational to boot.

Robert A. Selig, PhD
Holland, Michigan
August 2014

Preface

CERTAIN ASPECTS OF the campaigns of 1776 have received only passing mention in many history books. It is the purpose of this book to give more attention to lesser-known details. Students of The American War of Independence know that in getting cannon on top of Dorchester Heights, General Washington forced the British out of Boston without firing a shot, but how many know that the British had put a detailed counterattack plan in motion? Further still, how many know that Washington anticipated this plan and had a bold counter-counterattack plan. The Battle of Harlem Heights in Manhattan is another example. Usually given little attention, this small battle stopped what had been a rapid British advance in its tracks. Almost a month went by before British General William Howe resumed his attack. Seeds of the future victory the Battle of Trenton were planted there.

In this fictional account of the battles at Dorchester Heights and Harlem Heights, both famous historical figures and lesser-known common soldiers are included. Wherever possible, their actual recorded words have been woven into the story. (In reference to the end notes, if a particular phrase or sentence is an actual quote from a first-person account the entire quote will be listed. The whole paragraph may not have been drawn from that source—just the text that is noted. Some quotations have been altered slightly to better suit the story.) These quotations were taken from letters, diaries and pension accounts. Justus Bellamy, a sergeant in the Continental Army, is a key figure in the story. Much of what he wrote in his pension account is the basis for what I believe to be the most exciting chapter in the book. To receive a pension decades after the war, soldiers in the Continental Army had to submit a written account of their service to the pension board for approval. Only part of Bellamy's account is used. His whole story could be the basis of a movie in its own right.

As a George Washington impersonator, I have studied the man in depth since 2006. Between studying his life and performing first-person interpretations, I have gained a unique perspective on his character. Although this book is a historical fiction, I have used my knowledge of his character to inform his portrayal here and to make it as realistic as possible. From my earliest memory I have had a tremendous respect for George Washington. His courage, steadfastness, honesty, and faith are an inspiration to me. As I continue to study his life, my admiration for him continues to grow.

Acknowledgments

AS AN OVERVIEW of the period covered by this book, David McCullough's *1776* was a helpful resource. For the section on the siege of Boston, a 1976 Bicentennial *Boston Globe* insert was very helpful. Out of all the written accounts of that battle that I reviewed, that piece had the most in-depth information. Henry Phelps Johnston's *The Battle of Harlem Heights* was invaluable. Published in 1897, it is to my knowledge unmatched in its comprehensive account of the battle. My friends in the Revolutionary War reenactment community have always been helpful in my historical inquiries. Having actually taken part in light infantry drills at reenactments has given me an intimate knowledge of the maneuvers that provided me with unique insight while writing about the Battle of Harlem Heights.

Robert Child introduced me to the new world of eBook and direct paperback publishing. Fact-checking his book on Alexander Hamilton inspired me to write this book. Bucky Burruss and Garry Wheeler Stone had many helpful comments on the manuscript, as did Stuart Lilie. Dr. Robert Selig helped me to avoid many pitfalls that I might have fallen into without his help. On his advice I actually changed the ending of the book. Both Mr. Lilie and Dr. Selig added to the historical accuracy immensely.

Finally, I can't forget my sister, India. She edited the book. I have always admired her gift with the English language.

GEORGE WASHINGTON
AT WAR—1776

The Commander in Chief far from endeavoring to stifle the feelings of Joy in his own bosom, offers his most cordial Congratulations on the occasion to all the Officers of every denomination, to all the Troops of the United States in General, and in particular to those gallant and persevering men who had resolved to defend the rights of their invaded country so long as the war should continue. For these are the men who ought to be considered as the pride and boast of the American Army; and, who crowned with well-earned laurels, may soon withdraw from the field of Glory, to the more tranquil walks of civil life.

— George Washington,
Cessation of Hostilities, April 19, 1783

CHAPTER ONE

Remembrance

Mount Vernon, July 3ʳᵈ, 1785

A WEARY TRAVELER, William Cunningham, trotted up the road on his horse to George Washington's plantation. He was hoping to spend the night at Washington's home. It was the custom of the day for those of Washington's station to take in travelers, as there was no local inn. Cunningham had business in the area, and Mount Vernon was on his route. But it was more than a room for the night that Cunningham was looking for. He wanted an audience with the great hero of the war.

Cunningham finally had the great house in sight. It was not as pretentious as some European-style manors he had seen, but it had a charm all its own. As he came close to the house he was approached by a well-dressed Negro.* The man had a very erect posture and carried his head high. He had a regal air about him;

---

* This was the common name for an African American in the 18th century. It was not derogatory. A modern example is the organization the United Negro College Fund.

5

this was no field hand. He wore his cocked hat* in the military fashion, with the front corner placed very close to his left eye. He must have seen some service in the war. He walked with a slight limp, some old injury.

"May I be of assistance to you sir?" the man asked of Cunningham. His diction was perfect.

Cunningham, a bit surprised by the man's allocution, replied, "It is my hope to have lodging for the night."

"Very well, then. We can accommodate you. When the time comes for introductions, how shall I refer to you?"

"I am William Cunningham."

"I am Billy Lee. Please follow me to the stable, and I will see to your horse."

A small boy ran by as they walked to the stable. "That young lad certainly is in a hurry. Who might he be?" Cunningham inquired.

"That is young Master George Washington Parke Custis. He is the grandson of the General and Mrs. Washington. They call him 'Washy' for short. He does like to run about at play," Billy Lee shared. Washy had to have the Parke and Custis names to be eligible for the inheritance from each estate. He was the son of "Jacky" Custis, Martha Washington's son from her first marriage. Jacky died from a camp illness shortly after the surrender ceremony at Yorktown. He had desired to serve in the army.

At the stable, Cunningham dismounted and Billy Lee took the reins. There was a young Negro groomsman at work cleaning tack. Billy Lee approached the groomsman, "Jasper, see to this gentleman's horse and tack."

"Billy Lee," Cunningham interjected, "I have heard tell that the General has some of the horses he rode in the war kept here. May I see them?"

"Certainly, Mr. Cunningham" replied Billy Lee.

---

* What many people today refer to as the "tricorn" or "three-cornered hat" was called a cocked hat in the 18th century.

Billy Lee led Cunningham over to a pair of horses set apart from the others. "This is an opportune moment to get a close look at them. They have just finished their grain and will be released to their paddocks shortly," Billy Lee explained.

"Ah yes," Cunningham exclaimed, "His famous white horse."

"That is Blueskin. He was given that name as he has a bluish hue about his coat. He was also a fine foxhunting horse in his day. The chestnut is Nelson. He is 22 years of age now."

"I'm sure they have heard the roaring of many a cannon in their time," Cunningham commented.

"Blueskin was not the favorite," Billy Lee went continued, "on account of his not standing fire so well as the venerable old Nelson. The General makes no manner of use of them now; he keeps them here in a nice stable, where they feed away at their ease for their past services."

"Nelson is certainly a fine animal," Cunningham replied.

"The General accepted the surrender of the British Army at Yorktown mounted on Nelson," Billie Lee said with pride.

"If it is not an inconvenience, I would like to meet the General," Cunningham requested.

"I believe I know where the General is at the moment. I will take you to him."

They left the stable and approached one of the paddocks. Cunningham saw a man who had to be the General standing by a fence. Even though Washington did not know he was being observed, he stood as if he was posing for a portrait. It was just his way. It just so happened that it was Nelsons' paddock. Nelson was led out from the stable by the groomsman and then released. Upon entering the paddock Nelson sniffed at the ground, and then suddenly he was at the alert, with his head up high. He looked over at the General and broke into a canter toward him, neighing as he went. Just when it seemed Nelson was about to jump the fence he came to an abrupt stop in front of Washington. Nelson stood there motionless, proud to be caressed by the great master's hand.

Billy Lee and Cunningham approached the General.

"General," said Billy Lee, this is Mr. William Cunningham. He has requested our hospitality for the night."

"It is an honor to meet you, General Washington," Cunningham shared with humility.

"What brings you to this part of Virginia, Mr. Cunningham?" the General asked.

"My father is a Scottish merchant living in London. I have been tasked with collecting overdue debts. So far my travels have taken me from Canada to New York, Pennsylvania, Maryland, and Virginia. I am bound for North and South Carolina. As you can imagine, I am not very popular once I reveal the purpose of my visit to those who are indebted to my father," Cunningham explained.

"I can certainly commiserate, Mr. Cunningham. I have great difficulty collecting rents from tenants on my various properties. A defaulter is worse than a common pickpocket in my estimation," Washington shared with exasperation.

"General, I am a bit of an amateur historian, and if I am not mistaken, this is the 10th anniversary of the day you took command of the Continental Army at Cambridge, Massachusetts. If I may be so bold, I thought that it was a very clever move on your part to break the nine-month siege by seizing Dorchester Heights and using the guns from Fort Ticonderoga to force General Howe and the regulars out of Boston without firing a shot."

The General looked away. There was an uncomfortable pause in the conversation. Washington broke the silence, "I am aware of the anniversary." Washington reached into his vest pocket and removed his pocket watch. "You must excuse me, Mr. Cunningham. I have some business that must be taken care of at this time." As he walked away he stopped and turned, then said as an afterthought, "Please join us for tea, Mr. Cunningham. I am always curious to hear of news from afar."

Billy Lee, who was very intimate with the Generals' moods, knew in an instant what the problem was. He had noticed that the General seemed a bit more distant than usual and deep in thought throughout the day. In conversation the General looks you full in the face. The fact that he looked away when Mr. Cunningham brought up the anniversary explained everything. Billy Lee warned, "Mr. Cunningham, I caution you, it is not wise to bring up the subject of the war unless the General initiates the discussion. I rode by the General's side throughout the entire war, and we seldom speak of it."

Cunningham, somewhat shaken, replied, "I realized I had made a faux pas but could not understand what I had done that was offensive. I am grateful for your explanation. I shall endeavor to be more careful." Billy Lee showed Cunningham to his room.

———⊙———

IT WAS LATE evening when Cunningham, borrowing a lantern, went to check on his horse at the stable. Storm clouds had been moving in, and it was now starting to rain. Cunningham found his horse happily chewing on hay, with a full bucket of water off to his side. His horse had been well brushed. His tack was hanging neatly nearby. The bridle and saddle had been cleaned and oiled. The statement made earlier in the day by the Billy Lee to the groomsman, "See to this gentleman's horse and tack," held much more meaning than Cunningham realized at the time.

"Mr. Cunningham, come to check on your mount I see?"

Cunningham was startled to see the General standing in the stable doorway, also with lantern in hand. The afternoon tea with the General and Mrs. Washington had been quite pleasant. He even had the opportunity to spend more time with him earlier that evening, along with close acquaintances of the General. When Cunningham explained that his father had insisted on his keeping a diary of his travels, the General took immediate interest. Washington gave Cunningham a personal tour of his fields and gardens, allowed him into his private study, and showed him his large collection of wartime letters. Cunningham was relieved that he had gotten past that awkward moment with the General earlier in the day. But sensing the General was looking for time alone and not wanting to overstay his welcome, Cunningham thanked Washington again for his kind hospitality and wished him a good night.

There was another figure in the stable, this one skulking about. It was Washy. It was past his bedtime, but he had noticed his grandfather leaving the house at an unusually late hour and wanted to know where he was going. This was not his grandfather's routine. Washy was fascinated by his grandfather and often followed him. It was raining harder now. Washy watched his grandfather walk over to Nelson and run his hand down the horse's back. Nelson nickered.* This sentimental moment was shattered by a crash of thunder. The thunder had been almost simultaneous with the lightning, a very close strike. Washy nearly jumped out of his shoes. As he was standing on straw, and with the sound of the rain, his grandfather did not notice his presence. His grandfather's face had completely changed. He had that faraway look in his eyes that Washy had heard the other adults speak of. "Let him be," they would say in a whisper, "he is back in the war."

The burst of the thunder had brought Washington back to the siege of Boston. In his mind, he observed the great cannon bombardment that occurred before the Continentals took Dorchester Heights. Only those who have been in battle can know how real and vivid these flashbacks can be.

---

* "[A] horse uses his vocal cords but keeps his lips closed for this soft sound. It's usually (though not always) one of friendly recognition and welcome 'Hi! Good, you're here! Come talk with me!' coupled with an alert expression, raised head, ears pricked in your direction." www.equisearch.com/horses_care/health/anatomy/ eqsaying934/

CHAPTER TWO

The Seizing of
Dorchester Heights

Lechmere Point, Boston, Massachusetts,
March 4ᵗʰ, 1776, 7 P.M.

THE BATTERIES AT Lechmere Point on the mainland were being
worked by the gunners with great efficiency. The roar of the cannon
was deafening. This was the third night of the bombardment of Boston by the Continental Artillery. The waters of the Back Bay separated
them from the British Army, which occupied the city. The British answered back with their own cannonade. Abigail Adams reported being
able to hear the cannon fire from 10 miles away. The commander of
the Continental Artillery, Colonel Henry Knox, supervised the gun-
nery. Knox was a big man who carried himself with surprising agility.

Lieutenant William Rose commanded one of the cannons that
had just fired. Rose issued the firing commands: "Advance sponge!"
The gunner standing to the right of the muzzle dipped the sponge
end of his rammer* into the water bucket, removed it, and stood at
the ready.

"Tend vent!" Rose shouted. The bombardier, standing right behind

---

* See the end notes for explanations of the rammer, matross, fixed shot,
piece, and the lint stock.

the breech of the cannon, held his thumb (protected by a leather thumb-piece) over the vent hole. This sealed the vent hole and prevented any sparks from coming out.

"Spunge piece!" The gunner plunged his rammer, with the sponge end first, into the cannon barrel all the way to the end and then removed it. This cooled the barrel and prevented sparks from setting off the next cartridge prematurely.

"Handle cartridge!" The matross, standing well behind the cannon with the ammunition boxes, removed the fixed shot from his haversack and handed the cartridge to the gunner, who was standing to the left of the cannon.

"Charge piece!" The gunner with the cartridge placed it in the muzzle, with the powder-bag end entering first. He then gave the cartridge a push with the palm of his hand so that the rammer would more easily enter the barrel.

"Ram down cartridge!" The gunner to the right of the cannon, who held the rammer, pushed the cartridge to the end of the barrel, the breech.

"Prime!" The bombardier inserted the priming wire into the vent, puncturing the powder bag of the cartridge. After first returning the priming wire to the case on his belt, he unstopped the powder horn and poured gunpowder into the vent hole. The priming powder was now in contact with the powder in the cartridge.

"Take aim!" The bombardier checked the alignment of the barrel, and then backed away from the cannon.

"Fire!" The gunner brought down the lint stock onto the vent, igniting the powder. The force of the blast pushed the cannon back out of the ruts that had been dug for the wheels. The cannon ball plunged toward Boston.

Out of the night appeared General Washington, mounted on Nelson. He came to a sudden stop right in front of Knox. Billy Lee was by his side on his own mount, Chinkling. Not far behind was one the General's aides-de-camp, Major John Trumbull. Surprised, Knox saluted. Washington returned the salute.

"Well Mr. Knox, the guns you retrieved from Fort Ticonderoga are speaking loudly again this night."

Even though Knox had been serving under the General for many months now, he still held him in awe. The General and his horse functioned as if they were one creature, and Washington's commanding presence in the saddle was only slightly diminished when on foot. He had a powerful demeanor that was hard to explain without seeing it for oneself.

"Yes, General," Knox replied, "The guns are doing their work quite nicely."

A British cannonball roared across the Back Bay, passing over the heads of Lieutenant Rose's gun crew and just missing the three riders before it lodged into the nearby hill. It came so close that the energy of the cannon ball could be felt.

"Counter battery fire from the enemy," said Washington in a matter-of-fact tone of voice. The General looked at his watch, "We shall soon see if the three days of bombardment have served their intended purpose: to divert the enemy's attention from our real design. It's time we get over to Dorchester." The three riders were off.

———◈———

THE CONTINENTAL ARMY'S defensive lines on the mainland extended across a 10-mile arc to the west of Boston.[*] The Mystic River formed the northern boundary. The first of three peninsulas was Charlestown, connected by Charlestown Neck. This was also under British control. Charlestown was the location of the Battle of Bunker Hill. Lechmere Point was on the water, due south of Charlestown Neck. A narrow body of water, part of the Back Bay, left it very close to Boston's Barton's Point, less than half a mile

---

[*] During the war, Boston was technically a peninsula but felt much more like an island, connected to the mainland only by a narrow strip of land called Boston Neck.

away. The next town to the southwest was Cambridge. It was there, at the Vassal House, that Washington kept his headquarters. John Vassal, a loyalist, had abandoned the house.* The Charles River marked the southern boundary of Cambridge. The third peninsula included Dorchester Heights. The quickest route from Cambridge to Dorchester across the Charles was "The Great Bridge."

After crossing the Charles River on the Great Bridge, the trio went onto Brookline. At a crossroads they came upon a group of officers. "You have not seen the wagons pass this way, I take it, Gentlemen?" the General asked.

"No sir. Not a one."

"Where are those wagons? They should have passed this way by now," Washington stated with some exasperation. Addressing the officers, Washington inquired, "Does anyone know the whereabouts of General Gates?"

"Pardon me, General," a captain replied, "I saw him at his headquarters not one hour ago, studying maps."

"Studying maps!" Washington answered with annoyance. "That is an odd activity for our adjutant general to be engaged in at such a time as this." The group of officers chuckled under their breath. Where Washington was a man of action, Horatio Gates was sedentary.

"Will," Washington addressed Billy Lee, "Head out down that road and find John Goddard, the wagon master, and ascertain the reason for the delay. The Major and I will go onto Dorchester; find us there. We are behind schedule. Ride as if on the hunt!"

Without a word, Billy Lee wheeled his horse about and took off like a shot. He and his mount made an interesting pair. Each was slightly shorter than average height but powerfully built. Seeing that the road ahead was clogged with soldiers, Lee decided to take to the fields. He jumped a tall fence, dropped into a full gallop after

---

* The home would be purchased by Henry Wadsworth Longfellow in the next century.

landing, and then disappeared into the darkness. All who witnessed this stood amazed, their mouths hanging open. Trumbull spoke with astonishment, "Your Excellency, that fence must be at least four feet in height! It is the dark of night, and your servant rides with reckless abandon!"

Washington replied, "Will always accompanies me foxhunting. He is a fearless rider. Few are his equal in the saddle. Come now, Mr. Trumbull, it's time we move onto Dorchester."

The duo arrived at the mainland side of the causeway leading to Dorchester Heights. A group of soldiers were standing there, and Washington addressed a sergeant. "Sergeant, who might you be, and to which regiment do you belong?"

"Sergeant Amasa Soper of Kempton's Company, Marshall's Regiment, General."

Washington continued, "Sergeant, has there been word back from General Thomas? Has he taken the Heights?"

"No sir," the sergeant replied, "We have not heard from him since he stepped off."

Washington's plan was to have a three-day bombardment of Boston to distract the British while his troops took Dorchester Heights. A wall of bundles of pressed hay had been erected across the causeway to hide troop movements. On the third night, March 4, Brigadier General Thomas and 2,000 select men, the best of each unit available, started across the causeway of the Dorchester peninsula. Eight hundred men, mostly riflemen, took up positions along the shore of the Heights. Then came the carts with the entrenching tools. After that came the main working body under General Thomas, consisting of 1,200. These were the men who would be doing the hard work of assembling the fortifications.

Washington spoke again to the sergeant: "Do you have a fellow in your company who is fleet of foot?"

"Yes, General. Private Henry Cooke is very light on his feet."

"Send him up to the heights and have him report back as quickly as possible to me," Washington ordered.

Unexpectedly, like a lightning bolt shooting out of a cloudless sky, Billy Lee returned. He came from full canter to sliding stop, ending precisely at the General's side. Already a bit jumpy from all the noise of the bombardment, Trumbull's horse moved to the side violently. Long-time hunting companions, Nelson and Chinkling touched nose to nose in greeting. This was all old hat for them.

"General," Billy Lee exclaimed, "the lead wagon broke an axle. After repairs were attempted it was finally pushed aside. The wagons will be along presently." The group's attention was drawn to the Back Bay. The furious cannonade continued unabated from both sides. It was quite a spectacle.

Private Cooke returned, saluted, and reported to Washington. "General, the regulars [the British] seem unaware of our presence. General Thomas told me to tell you that the riflemen are in position along the shore, and the remainder of the troops have secured the heights. He is ready for the wagons." Private Cooke paused, but stood there as if he had more to say.

Washington inquired, "Is there something more private?"

Cooke replied, "It is very odd up there, very strange, General."

Getting a little exasperated, Washington asked, "Go on pray tell, what?"

"General, a thick fog has settled on the downward slope of the Heights, and yet at the summit the moon shines so bright it is almost as if it were day. The wind carries the noise of our activities away from the enemy."

"Private," the General explained, "it is quite plain; the hand of Providence has intervened for our cause. We can work on assembling the fortifications at the summit as if it were day, and our enemy in Boston will be blind and deaf to our activities." At that moment, the wagon train finally arrived.

The first group of wagons contained loads of barrels. Trumbull was puzzled, "Your Excellency, all the infantry have preloaded cartridges, as well as the artillery. Why are wagon-loads of gunpowder barrels being transported to the summit?"

"Mr. Trumbull, those barrels are filled with rocks and sand," Washington replied.

Trumbull was even more puzzled now, "Rocks and sand? I do not follow, General."

"The barrels will be placed in front of our fortifications. Should General Howe make the attempt to take the Heights from us, his troops will be hit with rolling barrels made heavy with rocks and sand. The Heights are steep and free of any trees or brush. Their climb uphill will be met with a devastating consequence."

Trumbull looked rather sullen and troubled. Washington continued, "Is something troubling you, Mr. Trumbull?"

Trumbull replied, "I am one of your aides-de-camp and this is the first I have heard of this."

"Only I know every facet of this assault," Washington explained. "I have not kept things from you alone. The enemy has ears everywhere. It is my duty as commander-in-chief to ensure the safety of the army by making sure my left hand doesn't know what my right hand is doing.

"I had been in command of the Continental Army for one only month when I learned in August that there was only enough gunpowder to supply 9 cartridges per soldier, only 36 barrels. I was informed of this by letter from Mr. Elbridge Gerry, the chairman of the committee of supply in Watertown. I was so struck that I did not utter a word for half an hour. I made it known that there were 1800 barrels of powder. I kept the truth to myself, sharing it with as few as possible. Had General Howe known how little powder we had, he would have attacked. I had to lie to save lives; it is a necessity in war. We must deceive the enemy at every turn."

Trumbull, looking more like himself, inquired, "But General, it is not the way of a gentleman to lie. Do you not find this very difficult?"

"Yes, Mr. Trumbull, it is against my nature. But remember the story of Rahab at Jericho.* She lied to the king of Jericho to save the lives of the Israelite spies. She gave them safe haven in her home and would not reveal it to the king when asked by him directly. Because of her actions, she and her family were spared from the destruction of

* The Bible, Joshua 2.

Jericho by the Israelites. She lied to save their lives. She is remembered in the scriptures* as one of the heroes of faith."

As the night wore on, hundreds of carts and wagons passed by and made the trip to the summit. Many of the carts made three trips, some four, for a vast quantity of materials had been collected, especially chandeliers† and fascines.‡ Three hundred and sixty ox teams were used. It was an enormous undertaking that required intricate planning. Digging fortifications on the summit was impossible, as the ground was as hard as rock—frozen solid, even though it was early March. The plan was to have hundreds of fascines assembled ahead of time, brought up to the summit, and placed in chandeliers. Hundreds of soldiers had labored in the days leading up to the assault, not knowing the purpose of their efforts. It had started with a discovery made by Lieutenant Colonel Rufus Putnam, a cousin of General Israel Putnam, who had read about the chandeliers in a military engineering book titled, *Muller's Field Engineer*. Given a structure to hold them, and with the fascines several feet thick, the quickly assembled fortifications would be not only bullet- proof but cannon-proof as well.

At the summit, one of Washington's most capable officers, Brigadier General John Thomas, was overseeing the work. The fortifications were taking shape, and the work seemed to go unnoticed by the British. Dorchester Heights was alive with activity, with hundreds of soldiers at work unloading wagons and assembling the fortifications. General Thomas was astounded to see his son running toward him, "John my boy, how in the world did you get past the sentries? What are you doing here? At 2 in the morning no less."

His 10-year-old son responded, "I wanted to be with you, Father."

---

* The Bible, James 2:25. For more on Washington and the Bible, see "Bible Verses" in the end notes.
† A chandelier is a stout wooden box made to hold the fascines.
‡ Fascines are bundles of branches. The bundles are 1 foot in diameter and are made up of branches 1 to 2 inches thick and 6 to 8 feet in length.

"Very well then, Son, remain here with me, but stay out from under foot!" General Thomas smiled in spite of himself. At 3 A.M. replacements relieved the initial assault force, whose men had been working hard at their labors since 7 P.M. the night before.

CHAPTER THREE

The Unveiling

General Howe's Headquarters in Boston, Province House,
March 5th, Sunrise

GENERAL WILLIAM HOWE was at breakfast with Captain John Montresor, who was considered the best engineer in the British Army. Howe respected Montresor; they had served together in the taking of Quebec in 1759 during the last war, with the French. Although a very capable officer in all facets of the military art, Montresor would not be promoted beyond captain, which was the highest rank that could be achieved by an engineer. Nonetheless, Montresor was the top captain for the engineers.

"This blasted bombardment over the past three nights, what do you make of it, Captain?" General Howe inquired.

"General," Montresor replied, "if we were dealing with the French, I would expect that this was preparation for a frontal assault on our position."

Howe replied with contempt, "I seriously doubt we have anything to fear from the Rebels [the Continentals]. Remaining on the defense is their way."

Montresor continued, "It is rather curious that they began their bombardment at 11 in the evening on the first two nights and yet began at 7 in the evening last night. Perhaps it is a diversion, a distraction, and they are attempting to hide some other activity from us."

"Well," said Howe, "if they are planning an attack, let them come. Our army will make short work of them."

General Howe changed the subject, "If only I had been given permission to quit this place before winter set in. Boston has little strategic value. By taking New York City we could gain control of the North River [Hudson River]. Denying the Rebels use of this vital waterway would cripple them. However, before we depart, I would like to strike a blow at the Rebels here. Captain, how can we dislodge the rabble in arms? The Rebel fortifications are for-midable. A frontal assault is still out of the question. The taking of Bunker's Hill* was too costly. The loss of half of my assault force continues to vex me."

After a brief pause, collecting his thoughts, Montresor replied, "General, we have further learned from prisoners that our third wave was successful, as the Colonials had run out of cartridges for their muskets. But I do concur that a frontal assault would be far too costly."

Howe took a swallow of tea, then said, "This only serves to compound my concern for the soldiers. There must be a better way."

"Perhaps the answer is right in front of us, General," said Montresor. "I am puzzled that the Rebels have not attempted to seize Dorchester Heights. It is open before us. If we were to take the Heights it could very well force them out."

"Captain, I have considered that. I know of the strategic im-portance of Dorchester Heights. I have purposely left it open to the

---

* The famous battle of Bunker's Hill (today called Bunker Hill) actually took place on Breed's Hill, a smaller hill closer to Charlestown and Boston Harbor. In his papers, Washington consistently referred to it as "Bunker's Hill," hence the confusion. For the sake of clarity, and since others followed Washington's lead in referring to this battle as the battle of Bunker's Hill, the battle will be referred to as such throughout the book.

Rebels, hoping they would make the attempt to take it, and thus spring a trap. We could push the Rebels off before they would be able to fortify. With that momentum we could then continue the assault into their other fortifications. Once we start them running away, panic would follow in their wake. In addition, placing cannon on the Heights would allow us to dominate the area."

General Howe finished the last morsel on his plate, took another sip of tea, and continued his remarks. "However, we are back to the same problem from where we started. I seriously doubt they will ever attempt to take the Heights. These colonists are amateurs; they lack boldness and audacity. Look at their successes thus far. In April they pushed our column back from Lexington and Concord through sheer weight of numbers and by shooting from behind trees and stone walls. The Rebels were simply an uncoordinated mob, not soldiers. At Bunker's Hill they fought only defensively, from behind fortifications. Once they saw our bayonets up close, they ran. This Washington is simply waiting for us to attack, as was done at Bunker's Hill. He lacks the imagination and intelligence to do anything else."

Montresor finished his tea in one long gulp and then replied, "General, if I may be so bold, it was quite clever and assertive of them to build the fortifications at Bunker's Hill overnight. They can't fight very well, but they dig like groundhogs."

"Your point is well taken, Captain. However, the ground is now as hard and impenetrable as rock. Even if they had the wherewithal to attempt taking the Heights and digging in, it would be impossible until the ground thaws."

"General, I would like to add, it is a mistake to underestimate Washington. I fought with him on the ill-fated Braddock expedition to take Fort Duquesne in the Ohio country from the French in 1755. The events along the Monongahela River on that dreadful day of July the 9th of that year will be forever burned in my memory. [Montresor took on a very solemn, distant look.]

"Our column was ambushed from three sides in a valley of a heavily wooded area. We could not see our Indian attackers, and yet they shot at us with deadly accuracy. They and their French allies had us trapped. Our men panicked, and many fired upon our own troops. I saw General Braddock receive the bullet that would prove to be fatal. The Indians specifically targeted our officers. I myself was wounded. In very short order all of the officers were killed or wounded save one, Washington. He was an aide-de-camp of General Braddock. He took command and organized a fighting retreat. He dashed about on horseback, rallying the men with no regard for his own personal safety. Two horses were shot from under him and yet he remained unscathed. Without his leadership the column may have faced annihilation. He was brave to a fault and demonstrated impressive leadership."

The breakfast conversation was interrupted by a knock on the door. "Enter," said Howe.

Captain Charles Stuart entered the room and reported, "Gentlemen, there has been a most startling occurrence with the Rebels. They have fortified Dorchester Heights overnight."

"That is impossible!" General Howe said with astonishment.

"Appeared more like magic than the work of human beings," Stuart added.

Howe passed through the doorway and addressed one of his aides-de-camp, Lieutenant Thomas Page, who was already at work, seated at a table. "Lieutenant Page, have a carriage brought around as quickly as possible!" Howe bellowed.

South Battery, a Gun Emplacement in Southeast Boston
Just Below the Wharves
(Location Providing a Direct View of Dorchester Heights)

GENERAL HOWE STOOD upon the parapet of the battery. He was joined by his engineering staff, Captains Montresor, Stuart, and Archibald Robertson. Several other officers were also present. "Astonishing, simply astonishing," Howe commented as he peered through his spy glass. "The Rebels have done more in one night than my whole army would have done in months!" Howe went on and said with authority, "We shall have a meeting of the staff within an hour's time. I expect a full report from the engineering officers on the extent and make up of these fortifications on the Heights. In the meantime, have the artillery fire upon them. I wish to ascertain if the artillery rounds can reach the Heights."

Standing among a group of junior officers, Lieutenant Carter commented, "The Rebels now command old Boston entirely; the enemy must inevitably be driven from thence, or we must abandon the town."

———————

Dorchester Heights, Small Fortification to the East of the Main Fortifications (Elevation: 112 feet)

TWO PATRIOT PRIVATES, brothers Asa and James Abbot, conversed. "I hear we have caused quite a stir among the inhabitants of Boston," said Asa. "They are all upon the roofs of their houses gawking at us. I was just over at the main fortifications and I overheard General Thomas speaking of it. I wish I had a spy glass, as he does." Both enlisted in the town of Andover, Massachusetts, on the same day, January 26, 1776.

"I hope those Redcoats pay us a visit up here. I am looking forward to it," James replied.

"You and I both James," said Asa. "Phillips's death must be avenged."*

At that moment, British cannons began firing from the Boston batteries. After a brief cannonade, the guns went silent again. "Asa, they can't hit us. Their cannon fall far short of our elevation. We have nothing to fear from their guns."

"James, look over at the main fortifications. It is General

---

* Phillip Abbot was killed at the Battle of Bunker's Hill on June 17, 1775.

Washington. He is addressing the men there. I wonder what he is saying."

When the General completed his speech, there was a loud cheer from those at the main fortifications. All the men out of earshot were very eager to know what the General had said. Finally, word traveled down the line. A man shared with the Abbots, "The General said to remember it is the fifth of March, and to avenge the death of your brethren."

"That is right," Asa said to James, "it is five years to the day of the Boston Massacre."

General Washington viewed the reaction of the British in his spyglass. General John Thomas was by his side. "Why General Thomas, the regulars are scurrying about in all directions. It appears we have caused the utmost consternation."

"Yes, Your Excellency, our overnight activity must be the talk of the town."

Washington closed his spyglass and handed it to Billy Lee. He then turned his attention to Thomas. "We shall soon see if General Howe is true to his word. We have learned from confidential sources that he would 'sally forth' if we were to take the Heights. We shall be ready to greet him, and furthermore, our boats are at the ready in the Charles for a landing north of Boston once General Howe departs with his assault force from the south."

General Washington had devised a complex trap. At the same time that General Howe launched his attack on Dorchester Heights, Major General Israel Putnam was to lead an amphibious assault with 4,000 men on the other end of Boston. Washington had planned since the beginning of his command at Cambridge to attack Boston with flat-bottomed boats. There were at least 60 boats big enough to carry 50 men each. This accounted for 3,000 men. The remaining 1,000 would be transported in smaller craft.

Large numbers of the flat-bottomed boats had been constructed earlier in the siege. The plan had previously been deemed too risky. But now, with a large British force attacking Dorchester Heights, only a small garrison would be left behind to guard Boston.

The signal for the attack was to be given from atop the Roxbury meeting house, which could be seen from Cambridge. The flotilla of small boats carrying the 4,000 men would be separated into two brigades to attack the northwest corner of Boston. One, under Brigadier General Nathanael Greene, would attack the West End at Barton's Point. The second, under Brigadier General John Sullivan, would attack at Boston Common and take Beacon Hill (south of Barton's Point). A body of troops would then fan out to the south and overwhelm the British manning the works at Boston Neck. The gates would then be opened to allow more troops in from Roxbury.

CHAPTER FOUR

The Gathering Storm

General Howe's Headquarters in Boston, Province House,
March 5ᵗʰ, 8:00 A.M.

GENERAL HOWE AND his full staff gathered in the main hall of Province House. Laid out on a table was a large map of greater Boston. There was a knock at the door. A lieutenant in the British Marines entered the room, saluted, and handed a note to Howe, "A dispatch from Admiral Shuldham, General." Howe quickly read the note, then conveyed its contents to his staff.

"The Admiral states that the Rebels have improvised a reversal which he finds alarming and unexpected. His ships cannot possibly remain in the harbor under the fire of the batteries from Dorchester Heights." Howe continued, "I would like a report from my engineers in regard to the fortifications on the heights."

Captain Montresor responded, "General, there are four redoubts* in total, two greater ones in the center and two lesser on either side. They must have either a very good engineer or access to a treatise on fortifications. They have employed chandeliers filled with fascines.

---

* A "redoubt" is an enclosed fortification, usually detached from a larger series of fortifications.

The depth of the walls is more than ample to stop solid shot. Of course, as we have already learned, that point is moot, as our guns cannot be elevated to reach that height. There appear to be some 20 cannon at the summit, most likely 12 and 18 pounders."

Captain Robertson shared his thoughts, "A most astonishing night's work. The materials for the whole works must have been carried by hundreds of wagons to the summit. A great deal of planning and preparation was required for this achievement. Last night's efforts alone must have employed from 15,000 to 20,000 men."

Howe said with assertion, "In a situation so critical, I have determined upon an immediate attack with all the force I can transport." There were no cheers in the room. All had witnessed the carnage of the assault on Bunker's Hill, it was still fresh in their minds. The faces of all the officers in the room took on a somber aspect.

Howe continued, pointing to locations on the map, "Five regiments are to embark immediately on five transports at Long Wharf. These, under the command of Major General Jones, are to proceed to Castle William to prepare to attack the Rebels from the east side of Dorchester Heights. Four elite battalions, two of grenadier and two of light infantry, will land at Nook's Hill to the west of Dorchester Heights. Two other regiments will provide support to this force. They will be prepared to embark at Long Wharf at 7 this evening. I will command this portion of the assault. Lord Percy and Major General Robertson will assist me. The landing boats from the ships will all start out at 9 this evening. The attack is to be made with the bayonet."

After a brief pause Howe continued, "There shall be a feint* toward Lechmere Point to throw the Rebels off as to our true intentions. Brigadier General Pigott is to remain in Boston with 600 men to guard against attack by the Rebels. I sincerely doubt we have anything to worry about with regard to a direct attack on

---

* A "feint" is a false demonstration or movement intended to fool an enemy into thinking you are attacking.

Boston. The town is to be scoured for scaling ladders for the troops to use to ascend the heights. All the ladders that can be procured are to be cut to 10-foot lengths."

Howe waited to see if there were any questions, "If there are to be no questions, let us be about our business."

As the officers filed out the door, Brigadier General James Grant paused to speak with Brigadier General Francis Smith (it would be hard to say which officer was more rotund). Grant, a member of the House of Commons, had boasted earlier in 1775 that with 5,000 British regulars he could march from one end of the American continent to the other. "There was never a doubt of General Howe's desire to attack." Grant shared with Smith.

"Indeed." Smith agreed.

Grant went on, "We had often talked over the subject and agreed that if the Rebels made that move to their right [to Dorchester], we must either drive them from that post or leave Boston. Everything has been prepared. As you have just seen, the assault plan was immediately formed, the redoubts to be stormed by the troops in column and not to load [their muskets,] since they might be under an absolute necessity of making use of their bayonets. We shall soon push the Rebels off the heights."

Smith replied, "Should we be forced to vacate, it would be rather inconvenient. This is a most inclement time of year for sea travel."

The officers who overhead the exchange shook their heads. Brigadier General Alexander Leslie said under his breath, "How does Smith keep getting promoted?"

Boston Long Wharf, 10 A.M.

THE WHARF WAS packed with troops embarking onto transports. Captain Montresor was supervising the loading of the artillery on the transports. As an artillery piece was hoisted away, he was approached by Captain Archibald Robertson. "May I speak with you privately, Sir?" Robertson inquired. Although they held the same rank, Montresor was Robertson's superior by years of service.

Montresor was busy at his work and preferred no interruption, but he sensed that Robertson had something important to say. "There is a quiet spot over there," he replied, pointing to an area of no activity near the wharf. The two men walked over.

Robertson shared his heartfelt concern, "I have already spoken with two lieutenant colonels, two majors, and three captains. We all concur. This assault is nothing less than suicidal madness. I think the most serious step ever an army of this strength in such a situation has taken considering the state of the Rebels' works* and the number of men they appear to have under arms. The fate of this whole army and the town is at stake, not to say the fate of America. Another bloodbath, as at Bunker's Hill, will be our ruin. We ought to embark immediately and get out of Boston."

Montresor replied, "Captain Robertson, it is true that I do not personally agree, but General Howe has told most everyone on his staff from the beginning of the siege that he would 'sally forth' if the Rebels were to move on Dorchester Heights. He cannot, as a gentleman and an officer, go back on his word. It is a matter of honor."

Robertson shot back, "Must men needlessly die for the sake of honor? The General respects your opinion. Can you speak with him?"

Montresor paused, looked away for a moment, and then looked straight at Robertson, "I am in agreement with your assessment. Your concerns echo my own. We shall put down this rebellion, but this is not the time or place. It must be on the ground of our own choosing. There will be an opportunity for me to speak with the General early this evening. For now, we must return to our work of loading the transports."

As Montresor and Robertson returned to the wharf, they noted the faces of the soldiers boarding the transports bound for Castle

---

* State of the Rebels' works – In his account, Robertson was referring to the strength of the fortifications on Dorchester Heights

William. They looked in general pale and dejected, having said to one another that it would be another Bunker's Hill affair, or worse.

Dorchester Heights, 10 A.M.

MAJOR JOHN TRUMBULL set down his spy glass on the rampart and began writing in his diary. "We saw distinctly the preparations which the enemy was making to dislodge us. The entire water-front of Boston lay open to our observation, and we saw the embarkation of troops from the various wharfs. We were in high spirits, well prepared to receive the threatened attack. We had at least 20 pieces of artillery mounted on [the Heights], amply supplied with ammunition. We waited with impatience for the attack, when we meant to emulate, and hoped to eclipse, the glories of Bunker's Hill."

Over at the smaller redoubt to the right flank, the Abbot brothers watched the activity in Boston. James said to Asa, "It appears that the whole British Army is loading onto transports in Boston."

"The lobster-backs shall make fine targets marching up this hill," Asa replied. "We may not even need our muskets. All we need do is to pull these ropes on the chocks* holding the barrels. It It will wreak havoc with them no doubt. Imagine their surprise when they see barrels by the dozen rolling toward them at break-neck speed. They will be powerless to do anything."

James, turning away from the scene before him and looking down to the ground, said to Asa, "I wonder what brother Phillip had in his thoughts when he saw the Regulars approaching at Bunker's Hill."

---

* Chocks – a triangular wedge to hold the barrels in place. A rope was attached to the wedge so that the chocks could be pulled out from behind the safety of the walls. Without the chocks, the barrels would roll downhill.

"We shall never know what he thought James," Asa replied. All we do know is that he stood his ground. Remember what the Crowley brothers shared with us. Phillip was last seen alive swinging his musket like a club against the Regulars as they penetrated the fortifications. In honor of his memory, we should also stand our ground."

At that moment their company captain, Frank Chamberlain, approached. "Attention to orders! Form up!" Chamberlain spoke with authority. The Abbott brothers came to attention, with their muskets at order arms,* along with the rest of the members of their company. Chamberlain continued, "As we can see plainly before us, the Regulars intend to take these works. You are not to fire unless given the command. Likewise do not, I repeat, do not release the barrels until commanded. If a single barrel is released prematurely it will bring our plan to ruin. Do not release the barrels until given the command 'Barrels away.' Only then are you to pull the ropes and release the chocks. Unless ordered otherwise, stay at your posts. Let me once again read an excerpt from the Commander-in-Chief's [General Washington's] orders from the other day:

" 'As the Season is now fast approaching, when every man must expect to be drawn into the Field of action, it is highly necessary that he should prepare his mind, as well as everything necessary for it. It is a noble Cause we are engaged in, it is the Cause of virtue, and mankind, every temporal advantage and comfort to us, and our posterity, depends upon the Vigor of our exertions; in short, Freedom, or Slavery must be the result of our conduct, there can therefore be no greater Inducement to men to behave well... Next to the favor of divine providence, nothing is more essentially necessary to give this Army the victory over all its enemies, than Exactness of discipline, Alertness when on duty, and Cleanliness in their arms and persons...'"

---

* Order arms is considered the position of attention. The musket butt is rested on the ground next to the right foot. The musket is held close to the body.

———————

Cambridge, by the Charles River, Noon

THE BANK OF the Charles was lined with flat-bottomed boats ready to cast off at a moment's notice. Hundreds of Patriot troops lingered nearby, waiting for the order to embark and make the amphibious assault on Boston. What had been an abnormally warm and pleasant day in the early morning had now turned cold and windy. Storm clouds had moved in. Washington, mounted on Nelson and accompanied by Billy Lee on Chickling, cantered over to a group of officers. Washington approached Major General Israel Putnam. Putnam saluted. Washington returned the salute and addressed Putnam. "General Putnam, I see all is ready for the assault on Boston."

"Yes, Your Excellency," Putnam replied. All is ready. The men are in high spirits and eager for a fight."

"I have found the same from the men at Dorchester Heights," said Washington. "Our officers and men appeared impatient for the appeal, and to have possessed the most animated sentiments and determined spirit."

Washington continued, "General Putnam, I see that the floating batteries* are in position."

"Yes, Your Excellency, three floating batteries will proceed in front of the other boats and keep up a heavy fire on that part of the town where our men are to land. The plan is well digested, and as far as I can judge from the cheerfulness and alacrity which distinguishes the officers and men who are to engage in the enterprise, I have reason to hope for a favorable and happy issue."

"Excellent, General Putnam," said Washington. "The time is fast approaching in which we are to execute this plan. I have received word that a large number of enemy transports have cast off

---

* A floating battery is essentially a gunboat carrying several cannon—in this case, a large flat-bottomed boat of similar construction to that of the troop-carrying boats. It would be rowed into position.

and are en route to Castle William. All that can be done now is to wait for the signal from Roxbury. Good day, General Putnam." Washington quickly turned and cantered off to the Vassal House, with Billy Lee by his side.

———◦⦿◦———

Dorchester Heights, 5 P.M.

THE TIDE HAD ebbed. The winds from the gathering storm blew harder and the direction had changed. It was now blowing west, directly against the British transports traveling from Boston to Castle William. Major Trumbull stood next to Brigadier General Thomas, who was observing the British transports with his spyglass as they struggled against the wind. Thomas remarked to Trumbull, "The sun is about to set. I can still just about see the movements of their transports. It is most likely they intend for a night attack, as troops are still en route. Many of their troops arrived on the island earlier in the afternoon. I sincerely doubt there will be an attack now. Many ships are being blown off course. Some of the smaller craft appear to be on the verge of being swamped by the violent seas. We must remain vigilant until morning, but I believe the danger of attack has passed. Please inform His Excellency that he should be able to rest easy this night."

CHAPTER FIVE

Evacuation

General Howe's Headquarters, Province House,
March 5th, 8 P.M.

CAPTAIN ARCHIBALD ROBERTSON paced nervously as he awaited the outcome of the staff meeting. General Howe had called the meeting at 7 in the evening to discuss the operation with some of his senior officers. The storm had increased in power. The winds were hurricane force and accompanied by snow and sleet. The door to Howe's office opened and several officers streamed out. Captain Montresor made eye contact with Captain Robertson as he left the office.

"Captain Robertson, please come with me," Montresor offered. The pair walked together to the main hall of the headquarters. They found a quiet corner. Montresor continued, "You can be at peace Captain. The assault has been called off." Robertson breathed a sigh of relief. Montresor explained further, "I advised against going off altogether. Lord Percy and some others seconded. General Howe said that it was his own sentiment from the first but thought the honor of the troops was concerned. In the event of the weather continuing to be boisterous tomorrow, it would give the enemy time to improve their works, to bring up their cannon, and put themselves into such a state of defense that he could promise himself little success by attacking them under all the disadvantages he had to encounter; wherefore he judged it most advisable to prepare for the evacuation of the town."

———◦◉◦———

Dorchester Heights, March 6th, 10 A.M.

THE ABBOT BROTHERS watched the British transports leaving Castle William en masse. James said to Asa, "Did we weather the storm all night here for no purpose?"

Asa replied, "I cannot think of a more miserable night in my life. I cannot recall a storm of such fury as this one. The Regulars must have come to their senses and called off the attack. Pity, I'm sure we would have given them a thorough thrashing." The brothers, who were looking at the activity in the harbor as they talked, did not notice that Lieutenant Isaac Bangs was standing right behind them.

"Quite a spectacle, is it not?" Bangs inquired. The Abbot brothers came to attention and saluted. Bangs returned the salute, "Take your ease." Bangs continued, "I could not help overhearing your conversation."

Bangs stepped up to the parapet and went on, "Why they had not done it that day, if they ever intended it, God only knows. For my part, I should have been willing to have received them either by night or day, as we had a tolerable cover from musketry, and as to their field pieces, they could not have brought them to bear because of the situation of the ground, our elevation being too great. Had they been so rash they would in all probability have found the 5th of March, 1776, more bloody on their side than Preston* made the same day in 1770 on ours. In fine, I can't think it was

---

* Captain Thomas Preston led the British troops who fired on the civilians at the Boston Massacre.

ever their design more than to make a parade. But they had good excuse; last night was the most violent storm of wind and rain mixed with snow and hail that ever I was exposed to."

Asa Abbot said with some surprise, "Lieutenant, do you mean to say that the whole thing was just for show, a spectacle?"

Bangs replied, "I do indeed. Their pride would not allow for our activities to go unanswered. A way had to be found to save face. But they must have also realized that the assault would have been futile against our fortifications. General Howe can now write a report to his superiors that an attempt was made but had to be canceled due to the storm."

Dorchester Heights, 4 P.M.

CAPTAIN FRANK CHAMBERLAIN approached. "Attention to orders! Form up!" The Abbott brothers took their places in the ranks. Chamberlain continued, "As we have all seen with our own eyes, the enemy has once again retreated into Boston. It is quite clear that their attack is off. The powerful hand of the Almighty has swept them away. Here are our orders from headquarters:

"Thursday the 7th, being set apart by the honorable the legislature* of this province, as a day of fasting and prayer, 'to implore the Lord, and giver of all victory, to pardon our manifold sins and wickedness, and that it would please him to bless the Continental Arms, with his divine favor and protection.' All officers, and soldiers, are strictly enjoined to pay all due reverence, and attention on that day, to the sacred duties due to the Lord of hosts, for his mercies already received, and for those blessings, which our holiness and uprightness of life can alone encourage us to hope through his mercy to obtain."

---

* The Massachusetts legislature — see the end notes for an explanation of fasting and prayer.

Washington's Headquarters, Vassall House, Cambridge, March 8ᵗʰ, Noon

WASHINGTON MET WITH his general staff. He sat at the head of the table, holding a letter in his hand. "Gentlemen, I have just received this note from the Ministerialists* in Boston. It came through our lines at Boston Neck by flag of truce. The paper was prepared by prominent Bostonians. It tells of having General Howe's assurances that the town will not be burned to the ground if they can be assured that they can depart Boston unmolested. I do not doubt their sincerity in departing, all of the mayhem of loading ships with all sorts of materials can be clearly observed from our view of the town. It is my recommendation that we let them leave; however, we should proceed with our plans to fortify Nook's Hill and place a battery there. Pressure must be brought to bear to give them all the encouragement to depart as quickly as possible. I must add that it is an unauthenticated letter, without an address. There is no obligation upon General Howe. Therefore, I propose that no official recognition should be afforded the appeal."

All the generals in attendance agreed. Washington continued, "As it was Colonel Ebenezer Learned who received the letter from the Ministerialists, I shall have him establish contact with them in the morning. He will explain that the letter was received by me, and that as it is an unauthenticated letter, I will take no notice of it. Any understanding between our camps will be strictly tacit."

Washington went on with new business. "Our next area of concern is what General Howe intends after he completes the evacuation of Boston. Regardless of the report from Boston that Halifax is the place of their destination, I have no doubt but that they are going to the southward of this, and, I apprehend, to New York. Many reasons lead me to this opinion; it is in some measure

---

* A term often used by Washington for the British military.

corroborated by their sending an express ship bound for York City [Manhattan] harbor, which ran aground at Cape Cod. Upon capture, the ship was boarded; she had a parcel of coal, 4,000 cannon shot, 6 carriage guns, and 3 barrels of powder. With this type of cargo en route to York City, it can only mean that they are planning to seize it.

"A further indication of General Howe's intent on York City, is the naval activity in the harbor. In General Lee's* last dispatch before giving up command of the York City defenses, he summarized the enemy's naval activity in the harbor.

"Before his arrival with 3,000 men, the inhabitants of the city were freely conducting business with the enemy. General Lee cut off all supplies of fresh provisions to the enemy vessels. Several batteries were put in place, forcing the His Majesty's ships to deeper water. The Ministerialists did not fire upon our batteries, perhaps out of concern for damaging the property of Loyalists in the city.

"Based on these observations, it is quite clear that General Howe is planning to capture York City. It is an excellent harbor, with access to the North River [the Hudson]. If the Ministerialists gain full control of the North River, our country will be severed in two. We must make preparations to leave immediately for New York as soon as General Howe has vacated Boston. Upon arrival we must be conscious to treat the citizens as our own, even though it appears that the majority are clearly Loyalists. I shall hold the Riflemen and other parts of our Troops in readiness to march at a moment's warning and let my movements be governed by the events that transpire, or by such orders as I may receive from Congress, which I beg may be ample and forwarded with all possible expedition."

---

* General Charles Lee was the highest ranking officer under Washington in the Continental Army. On March 1st, Congress directed General Lee to take over the Southern Department at Charleston, South Carolina.

CHAPTER SIX

Interlude

THE BRITISH DEPARTED Boston on March 17, 1776. They did in fact go to Halifax, Nova Scotia. Washington, with most of the army, departed Boston for New York on April 6. Washington was correct in his assumption that the next target of the British would be New York City. He was wrong about the timing. Howe, smarting from his inglorious defeat by the Rebels, was to get his revenge. In June and July, a massive British fleet arrived in New York Harbor, consisting of 30 ships of the line (battleships,) 30,000 soldiers, 10,000 sailors, and 300 supply ships. Hessian mercenaries were part of the assault force. It seemed to those at the time that there was a virtual forest of masts in the harbor. In July, Staten Island was taken by the British.

Washington had spent considerable effort fortifying Long Island and New York City since he arrived in April. The British struck Long Island on August 27, 1776. Diversionary forces demonstrated*

---

* Demonstrated: British and Hessian troops maneuvered and fired upon the Continentals and made it look as if they were going to charge the fortifications. This was only a ruse to attract attention away from the real assault.

in front of the American lines while General Henry Clinton attacked the flank. In a bold night march, Clinton was able to exploit a gap in the lines and attack the unsuspecting Continentals in the rear. There were some acts of supreme bravery among the Continentals—the Delaware and Maryland troops were examples—but most fled in panic. The Battle of Long Island ended in a rout.

The Continentals fled to the fortifications at Brooklyn Heights to the extreme west of Long Island. Their backs were to the East River just across from New York City. Howe ordered a stop to the advance just short of the Brooklyn Heights fortifications. Critics of General Howe have long complained that he should have pressed the attack on the same day. Once you have your enemies on the run, don't give them time to pause and regroup. Was Howe afraid of repeating the bloodbath of Bunker's Hill? Others have theorized that his objective was not to annihilate the Continental Army but to force its surrender. He did initiate peace talks before the battle. It is very likely that he did not want lives lost needlessly on either side. In any case, Howe was not idle. In a textbook siege maneuver, he had trenches dug closer and closer to the Rebel lines at Brooklyn Heights. He would be able to bring up mortars and howitzers to pummel the Rebel lines and without risking a frontal assault over open ground. With the Continental Army having its back to the river, the Royal Navy being in control of the waterways, and the Continentals being hopelessly out numbered, perhaps Howe thought Washington would surrender—this would have seemed logical.

As at many points during the war, Washington didn't do what the British expected. Yet they never seemed to fully comprehend this fact until the war was almost over. Lord Cornwallis developed a grudging respect for General Nathanael Greene, who wore him out in several battles leading up to Yorktown in 1781. Cornwallis complained, "Greene is as dangerous as Washington. I never feel secure when encamped in his neighborhood."

On August 29, Washington decided to evacuate. With the help of Colonel John Glover and his Marblehead Regiment, one of the most amazing feats of the war was accomplished. All of the men in Glover's regiment were able seamen. Washington's entire army of 9,000 was evacuated overnight across the East River to Manhattan. It took many round trips. Yet this was all done under the very noses of the British Army and Navy. The job was not complete by sunrise. But once again, as at Dorchester Heights, Providence was with Washington. A heavy fog settled in and provided a screen for the activities. By 7 A.M. Washington boarded one of the last boats and crossed. The British were dumbfounded when they discovered what had transpired.

Of course, wars are not won by brilliant evacuations, but the army was saved to fight another day. General Howe waited two weeks and then landed at Kips Bay in Manhattan on September 15. After a furious cannonade from the British Navy, the assault troops landed unopposed. Shaken by the cannon fire, and carrying in their minds the memory of the recent defeat at Long Island, the militia fled at the sight of the British and Hessians. Not only did they flee, but many threw down their muskets and cartridge boxes to speed their escape.

Ironically, Washington had ordered New York City to be evacuated that day. Some military stores were already on the move out of the city when the British landed. But with the British and Hessian troops moving inland from Kips Bay, the heavy guns and 4,000 Continentals under General Putnam in the city were in grave danger of being cut off.

CHAPTER SEVEN

The Chase

Washington's Headquarters, Colonel Roger Morris's House,
Harlem Heights (Upper Manhattan),
September 15th, 1776

IT WAS LATE afternoon. Washington entered his office and shut the door. He poured a glass of water out of a pitcher, took a long drink, and sat down at his desk. He held his head in his hands, pondering the horrors of the day. He whispered to himself in disgust, "Are these the men with which I am to defend America?" There was a knock at the door. He gathered his composure and said, "Enter."

Lieutenant Colonel Joseph Reed approached the desk. "General, I'm glad to see you. Others and myself were concerned." Washington had nearly been captured in the morning near Kip's Bay, early in the invasion. He could not stop the Connecticut Militia from running away from the enemy. He sat on his horse, frozen in discouragement, until his staff came on the scene and led his horse away by the reins. The British light infantry stopped their advance, as if confused. It was a very close thing.

"Mr. Reed, I appreciate your concern. Has there been any word about General Putnam and his men?"

"No sir. They received the order to evacuate the city, but it is

47

feared that they may have been cut off by the rapidly advancing British and Hessians heading west."

Washington rose from his chair and paced about the room. He then speculated, "If they took the Old Post Road going north through the center of the island, General Putnam and his men will most certainly be cut off. Even the Bloomingdale Road may not be far enough west. He has 4,000 men we cannot afford to lose. Have Will saddle up Nelson; Blueskin is spent. I shall go forth and find out for myself."

Reed replied, "Is that wise General, to travel alone?"

"Do not worry, Mr. Reed. Nelson is a fine mount; he will get me out of whatever trouble I may encounter."

———⊙———

Southwest of Harlem Heights, Same Day

LIEUTENANT COLONEL SAMUEL Birch,[*] commander of the British 17th Light Dragoons, personally led a troop of his regiment on patrol. At the last fork he had divided the troop into two groups of 20, so as to cover more ground. Earlier in the day, a Loyalist citizen had informed him that the last remaining Rebels had left the city, were heading north, and would most likely be traveling on the Bloomingdale Road that was to the west, near the North River. Finding no sign of Rebels on the Bloomingdale Road, the dragoons turned east. Unbeknown to them, as they were unfamiliar with the area, General Putnam and his column had taken a less-traveled road west of the Bloomingdale Road and closer to the North River. The 17th Light Dragoons wore brass helmets with the distinctive emblem of a skull and crossbones on the crest—a death's head. Their regimental motto was, "Death or Glory!" Birch had his group of 20 mounted dragoons arrayed in five sections, four to a section.

---

[*] Birch was in command of the 17th during the New York campaign.

General Washington was heading west toward the Blooming-dale Road, about 2 miles southwest of Mount Morris (his headquarters), on his way to find General Putnam and his column. Washington turned a bend in the road and found himself running head on into the 17th Dragoons. The dragoons came to a halt, as did Washington; both were surprised by the encounter. "It's a high-ranking Rebel officer," shouted Birch. "Second section, break out of the column and take him!" Four dragoons separated from the column. Washington paused briefly and smiled. He then wheeled Nelson about and sprinted off in the direction from which he had come. For the first time in his life, he was the hunted. The veteran fox hunter found himself to be the fox.

Washington quickly formulated an escape plan. All the dragoons were mounted on thoroughbreds. Nelson was surefooted and very quick from a standstill, but over distance would be overtaken by the thoroughbreds. The horse was very fit at age 12, but no match for a thoroughbred half his age. Washington knew he could not get away on the road. He decided to take to the fields. A surveyor by training, Washington was always aware of the topography as he traveled. A keen foxhunter, he also was in the habit of observing the ground to consider how it might be traversed on horseback. Having been on this road several times before, he recalled a field that was close at hand. It was enclosed by woods and had a narrow trail at the far end.

The four dragoons were closing in on Washington. The rest of the column followed from behind, but at a more relaxed pace. The field came into view. Heavy brush blocked the way except at one spot, where there was a downed tree. Off to the far left Washington could just barely make out the trail. He jumped the downed tree and swapped to the left lead* in midair. Washington stayed on the left lead as he headed straight for the wood line far to the right of the trail. The four dragoons jumped the downed tree in pairs, one pair followed by the other. Sergeant Jones, proud of having the fastest

---

* See the end notes for more information on horses and lead changes.

horse in the regiment, broke away from the other three. He came up on the left of the Rebel officer, to grab his reins. He wanted to impress his commander by taking the man prisoner by himself.

The rest of the column jumped the tree and came to a halt in the middle of the field. Birch saw no clear way out of it. "Lieutenant Loftus," Birch commented, "it appears our entertainment will be short-lived. Our quarry will be too easily captured. Did this pathetic colonist really think he could outride some of the best horsemen in England?" They had no idea who they were up against. The dragoons were about to get a riding lesson they would not soon forget. Their contempt would be their undoing.

As Sergeant Jones accelerated, he leaned forward and reached out to grab the reins. Too focused on that objective, he failed to realize how close he was getting to the tree line. The head of Jones's horse was just behind Nelson's rump. Suddenly, in one clean and swift movement, Washington made a hard left turn and cut off his pursuer. The unexpected movement caught the sergeant completely off guard. Jones's horse was 3 years old and a little green, and thoroughbreds can be jumpy. Consequently, the horse panicked as it came upon the tree line. Part of a horse's training is getting it accustomed to balancing a rider on its back. Jones's horse forgot about its rider and thought of itself. The horse broke hard to the left to avoid running into the trees. Instinctively, it kept following the horse in the lead. Jones had been leaning forward in an unstable position, and the sudden move threw him out of the saddle. His foot got caught in the stirrup iron. Now, dragging the man, the horse panicked further. Being flight animals, horses try to run from danger.

Private Gridley, who had been riding side by side with Sergeant Jones before Jones had galloped ahead, called out to the other two dragoons. "Keep after the Rebel. I'll stop Jones's horse!" Gridley rode alongside of Jones's horse, grabbed the reins, and stopped the horse as the other two dragoons galloped past. Gridley yanked the stirrup leather out of the keeper and freed Jones. Privates Smith and Derry bore down on the Rebel officer. Smith pulled ahead on the left to grab the reins, and Derry approached from the right to box Washington in. All three riders were very close to the tree line, but Derry was the closest and had to keep raising his hand to prevent the ends of branches from hitting him in the face. His position also obscured his view.

Washington was now within a few strides of the trail, which was just barely visible through the trees. Washington made another lead change, swapping to the right lead. Making a hard right turn, he plunged into the trail entrance, ducking his head to avoid a stout tree branch. Smith, on the left lead, couldn't make the right turn into the trail. He brought his horse to an abrupt stop to avoid hitting a tree. Derry, after being hit with the last branch that had been obscuring his view, burst onto the scene, totally unprepared. Having attempted to make the turn, Smith had stopped perpendicular to Derry's approach. Derry crashed into Smith's side, and in the collision Smith's horse fell over, pinning its rider's leg. Smith knew his leg was broken. Derry flew head over heels out of the saddle, landing in the brush. He cracked his jaw on a rock. Having freed Jones, Gridley now became even more furious as he observed the ill fates of Derry and Smith. He galloped into the trail. He saw the stout tree branch that Washington had avoided, but too late. He was knocked unconscious and fell off his horse.

Lieutenant Colonel Birch was dumbstruck. The four dragoons he had sent out to capture the Rebel officer were now on the ground, seriously injured. "Lieutenant Loftus! Take two sections and go after him. I no longer care about capture! Shoot him!" Birch bellowed. As the eight dragoons galloped past Birch, he shouted out commands. "Private Lilie, find the rest of the troop and bring them here. We will have to set up a defense until we can get our wounded out. Private Griffin, get back to our lines and get a carriage with a fast team. It must be large enough to hold our wounded. Bring along the reserve troop. Off with you!" Lowering his voice and speaking to himself, Birch said with disgust, "I cannot believe it. What a debacle."

Washington came to a halt and turned around to see if they had given up the chase. His question was soon answered with the sound of thundering hooves. The trail was most likely used for hauling firewood by the farmers. It started off fairly straight and level, but beyond the point where Washington had halted, the trail wound and meandered uphill, following the contours of the land rather than a straight line. Washington was off again with not a moment to lose—now with twice as many dragoons hot on his heels.

In the fury of pursuit, Lieutenant Loftus ended up in the middle of the pack. Private Winchester was in the lead. With Washington's loss of momentum from the halt, and with the straight and level portion of the trail open to them, the dragoons closed the gap quickly. Washington sprinted off, entering the winding part of the trail. Left turn, right turn, left turn, right turn, ducking low-hanging branches as he galloped up the hill. Winchester was close enough now that the dirt kicked up from the hind hooves of Washington's horse was hitting him in the face. Winchester's horse was no match for the sure-footed Nelson. Getting its hoof caught in a root, the horse instantly went lame. Winchester dug in his spurs, but it made no difference—the horse would not resume the chase. The dragoons bunched up behind the injured horse. "Get off the trail, Winchester!" yelled Loftus. Winchester was loathe to give up the pursuit, but he got off the trail.

Washington reached the top of the hill and galloped across the open ground at the summit. The trail continued down the other side of the hill. The descent was quite sharp, much steeper than the trail on the ascent. He leaned back in the saddle to get pressure off Nelson's front legs. Too much weight on a horse's front end on a declining slope can cause the horse to trip. Back on level ground, Washington encountered a gully with a stream running through it. There was about a 5-foot drop to the water. With his surveyor's eye, Washington estimated the distance across to be between 14 and 16 feet. An extreme jump, but he knew his horse could do it. Without hesitation Nelson jumped the gully. Private Nash, who was right behind, had a very different result with his horse, which came to an immediate halt, refusing the jump. The dragoon went flying over the horse's head and landed in the muddy water below. Loftus halted at the edge and exclaimed, "Damn! Who in God's name is that man!" The remaining six dragoons crossed the gully the hard way, going down in, and wading across. Private Nash broke a few ribs as he landed in the stream and had to stay behind. Private Darby held the horse's reins long enough for the injured, muddy, sopping-wet dragoon to take hold of them. He then bolted off to join the others on the hunt.

Always cognizant of his location, as if looking at a map, Washington knew he was taking a shortcut that would lead him back to the road that would take him to the American lines. On exiting the trail he found himself in another field. At the far end he viewed a tall fence. The dragoons burst out of the trail into the field. Seeing the instrument of so many injuries and indignities just ahead, they spurred their horses on. Loftus drew his first pistol out of his saddle holster and brought it to full cock. Fortunately for Washington, pistols were terribly inaccurate, except at very close range. As Loftus closed the distance he took a shot. It whizzed by Washington's ear. He recalled his first experience as a young man in battle. He had commented at the time, "I heard the bullet's whistle, and, believe me, there is something charming in the sound."

As Washington closed in on the fence, he slowed down from the gallop to a more controlled canter. He had to set the distance right for Nelson. It was a tall fence; the jump had to be set up properly. To remain at the gallop would force Nelson to jump too soon. Leaving the ground too soon would force the horse to jump farther and higher to clear the fence. He would not be able to clear this high fence in that way. Even if the fence could be cleared at that speed, the jump would be flat; the horse could get a leg hung up on the fence and flip over. Loftus pulled the trigger on his second pistol just as Washington and Nelson left the ground. The bullet hit the highest pole on the fence as Nelson cleared it.

Corporal Wilson and Lieutenant Loftus were first to the fence. It was a height that they would never consider jumping. Wilson said with amazement, "This fence must be 5 feet in height. That fellow can really ride!" Loftus replied, "I want that horse! You two, dismount and tear down these fence poles. Corporal Wilson, exchange your pistols with mine. I want another crack at him."

CHAPTER EIGHT

Desperate Ground

An Isolated Redoubt, West of the Old Post Road South and Harlem Heights, September 15th

NOT FAR FROM spot where Washington and Nelson made their jump, a desperate battle raged near Harlem Heights. The Continental Army was in retreat, heading for the Heights. A small unit of 70 men from Colonel Thaddeus Cook's regiment were tasked with being the rear guard of the last baggage train of wagons leaving the city. Now these Connecticut men found themselves cut off from their regiment and surrounded by the rapidly advancing British and Hessian troops. The detachment threw together a rough fortification to fight for survival. "Where are our officers!" yelled Private Stroup.

Sergeant Justus Bellamy looked around and saw Stroup was right. With all the firing going on, the officers had not been missed until now. Thinking quickly, as was his way in an emergency, Bellamy called out, "Our only chance to get out of here is to charge at them to the north. At the next volley, we will attack. We will pounce upon them in their own smoke. Save your bullets till we get right up to them. Don't 'Huzza'* until then. Prime and load†! You lads toward the back, form a second rank behind when we step off. Be ready to use your musket butts." Bellamy was well respected in the regiment. What he said made sense. The soldiers had heard rumors of Continentals captured at the Battle of Long Island living in horrible conditions in prison ships in the harbor. They were not about to suffer that fate.

As soon as the British fired the next volley, the Connecticut men charged. When they were within a few strides of the British, they yelled "HUZZA!" Always viewing Continentals with contempt, the British were stunned. They were caught in the midst of reloading and were totally unprepared to face a bayonet charge. When their bayonets were about to touch the British in the first rank, who were in the kneeling position, the Connecticut men fired from the hip. They plunged their bayonets into the second British rank even before the first rank had fallen. Just as Bellamy twisted his bayonet into the stomach of an enemy soldier, Corporal Garnett Howard, right behind Bellamy in the Continental second rank, sent his musket butt with extreme force into the face of a man in the British third rank.

The suddenness and ferocity of the charge caused the few remaining men in the British company to scatter. It was as if they had been overrun by a cattle stampede. The Connecticut men ran north for about 40 yards, and Bellamy ordered a halt. "Second rank [whose muskets were still loaded], to the right about face! Cock your firelocks! Present! FIRE!" This maneuver accomplished two things. More lead was poured into the British, and the smoke obscured the attackers from view. The Connecticut men did not pause again but kept running to make good their escape from the other British units in the area.

Entering a small wood, running across fields, and finally a road, they broke into a larger wooded area and took a breather. The

---

* Huzza: A cheer from the 18th century. Soldiers would yell "Huzza" when charging the enemy with the bayonet.
† Prime and load: See the end notes for a detailed explanation.

sounds of the battle had subsided. It did not appear that they were being followed. Going deeper into the woods, all was quiet. The men proceeded with stealth, not knowing who they might run into. Suddenly, shots rang out behind them, from where they had come. "Those sound like pistol shots," Private Johan Selēn commented.

"Stroup," said Bellamy, "you're light on your feet. Go back to the tree line and take a look. The rest of us are going into the clearing ahead. Report back as soon as you've seen something." Just as Private Stroup got to the woods' edge, he saw the six dragoons in pursuit of Washington ride by. He recognized the distinctive brass helmets of the 17ᵗʰ. The General had ridden by only moments before, but the private never saw him. Stroup sprinted back to his unit, where the men, now in the clearing, were drinking from their canteens and seeing to their muskets with the pick and wisk.*

Stroup called out excitedly, "Dragoons! There are six of them. Some have their pistols drawn. They are heading east in a hurry."

Bellamy thought quickly, "That explains the pistol shots. But why were they shooting? Is it some kind of signal? Six of them you say? They must be scouting, looking for weaknesses in our lines. The road they are on will take them southeast before they cross the Old Post Road. I know where we are now. I passed by this way just the other day. We are just short of the fork of the Old Post Road and the Kings Bridge Road. If they are looking for our Army, they will head north. I know where there is a bend in the road by the fork, where they won't see us until the last minute. We will deny them both roads by stopping them at the fork. If we step lively we can barricade the road and be waiting for them. Follow me! March-March!"† They took off at a run.

---

* Pick and wisk: The pick is used to clear the touch hole and the wisk or brush to clean the pan; both the hole and the pan get fouled with burnt gunpowder.
† March-March is the 18ᵗʰ-century military command equivalent to "double-time."

In a few minutes they were on the Old Post Road at the spot Bellamy had in mind. The men quickly gathered some fence poles and dead branches and set up a crude barricade. Bellamy gave his final orders, "Form two ranks! First rank, kneel and prepare to repel horse. Prime and load! Second rank, prime and load! Cock your firelocks!" The first rank held their bayonets at a 45 degree angle, with the muskets butts firmly on the road. This formation would present a wall of bayonets that no horse would cross. The second rank, just behind, was standing and ready to fire. The only next step was to pull the trigger. The whole road was covered by the 70 men. The dragoons would not get past.

Washington tore down the road at a full gallop, but once again, the young thoroughbreds, bred for racing, were gaining on him. He was very close to the American lines, but he was running out of time. Another pistol shot, then another. Loftus waived the other dragoons forward to fire their pistols. "Shoot the man, not the horse!" Washington made a hard left turn onto the Old Post Road. As the dragoons made the turn, they lined up four abreast. With eight shots among them, they couldn't miss. Lieutenant Loftus and Corporal Wilson brought up the rear.

The Connecticut men heard the sound of the galloping horses bearing down on them. Even with a wall of steel [bayonets] in front, it is very intimidating to be confronted with a group of cavalry coming at you at a gallop. The men in the front rank, in the position of "Repel Horse," were resolute and held their ground. "The timing has to be right," Bellamy yelled, "Don't fire until I give the command." The rear rank was at the "Cock your firelocks" position, with the musket cocked, ready to fire, and held close to the body, perpendicular to the ground. "Present!" Bellamy commanded, and the men brought their muskets to the shoulder and leveled them.

At that moment Washington burst around the bend in the road. "As you were—it's General Washington! Hold your fire!" Bellamy quickly put down his musket, ran to the center of the ranks, and yanked out two men from the rear rank and two from the front. "Form a third rank! Make room for the General! He is coming on fast! He is going to jump the barricade! " It was again a very close thing. Right down to a split second. As Washington came within a few strides of the barricade, Bellamy gave the command, "FIRE!" At the precise moment that the muskets released the bullets, Washington was in the air, flying over the barricade. All four dragoons in front were riddled with bullets and fell from their horses. Loftus and Wilson just missed the carnage. They came to a sliding stop, wheeled about, and galloped off from whence they came. Guided by their herd instinct, the riderless horses followed the other two.

Washington petted Nelson on the neck and said, "Well done, old boy." Then Washington addressed the men, "I am in your debt. To what regiment do you belong?"

"We are Connecticut men from Colonel Thaddeus Cook's regiment, General," Bellamy answered.

"How did you come to be at this location?" Washington inquired. Bellamy related their adventures. "Come on now, let us march back together to our lines," Washington said.

As they all walked back, Washington thought over the day's events. He had held such distain for the Connecticut Militia after their cowardly retreat at Kip's Bay. And here before him were brave, stouthearted men from the same state. Knowlton's Rangers, also from Connecticut, had performed admirably on dangerous missions in Boston during the siege. With the right leadership and training, the men would fight. As much as the people of this new country feared a standing army, Washington had long known that a professional army was necessary to winning this war. There had to be a new, highly trained army along European standards. Washington also considered how he might use the contempt the British felt toward the Continentals as a weapon against them. Perhaps tomorrow the day would go differently.

———※◎※———

LOFTUS AND WILSON, on their mounts, retraced their steps back to the gully. They held the reins of two riderless horses. Two of the four horses were badly wounded and had to be left behind. Once the two dragoons crossed the gully and rode back up to the summit of the hill, they were greeted by a dismounted sentry from their regiment. He had his carbine* at the ready.

As Loftus and Wilson continued past the sentry, they saw two more dismounted dragoons hidden in the wood, ready to support the lone sentry. Further down the trail, four horses were tied to trees, with a dragoon guarding them. This group of four was an advanced picket, or sentry post. They could alert the rest of their party very quickly should there be an approach by the enemy. Two more dismounted sentries greeted the pair as they entered the clearing where the debacle had begun. A strong defensive perimeter had been set. Lieutenant Colonel Birch knew what he was doing. The dragoons were in enemy territory, separated from the main army. It was still a very fluid situation.

As Loftus and Wilson entered the road from the clearing, they saw the injured dragoons being placed in a carriage. Private Derry was still unconscious. Birch was supervising. The other half of the troop had returned, and the reserve troop was also present. Pickets had been set up a hundred yards west and east of their position on the road. Another picket was set to the south, at a farmhouse. As they approached, with two riderless horses in tow, no one needed to ask why. Birch spoke to Loftus and Wilson, "Neither of you is to speak of this incident until further notice. Lieutenant Loftus, I will expect a full report this evening at our new headquarters in the city. Corporal Wilson, pick a private to accompany you. Go back to the city and find out where the surgeon general has set up hospital. Make preparations for our injured. Take those two horses and find suitable stabling for the regiment near General Erskine's headquarters." At that moment the pickets to the south, at the farmhouse, reported the approach of elements of the main army.

---

* See "Dragoon weapons" in the end notes.

CHAPTER NINE

Revenge

Lieutenant Colonel Birch's New Office, Brigadier General Sir
William Erskine's Headquarters, Lower Manhattan,
September 15th, Late Evening

LOFTUS KNOCKED ON the door. "Enter," said Lieutenant Colonel
Birch, who was seated at a table. "Lieutenant Loftus, what happened?"

Loftus responded, "Sir, we almost had the Rebel officer when we
were ambushed. The four men must be dead. They faced a hailstorm
of bullets. Their horses followed us for a distance until we found that
two had been shot. We had to put them out of their misery, sir."

Birch slammed his fist down on the table. He reached for a
piece of paper out of a pile and stood up. "Here is my report, let
me read it to you."

> Sergeant Jones: Dragged from stirrup iron. Shoulder dis-
> lodged; damaged ankle may not heal.
> Private Smith: Broken leg, crushed under horse.
> Private Gridley: Thrown from horse, broken jaw.
> Private Derry: Knocked down by striking head on tree
> branch, still unconscious.
> Private Nash: Thrown from horse, broken ribs.
> Two horses lame, one may not heal.

"And now you add further casualties to the list! Nine dragoons out of action! Four believed dead! Two more horses lost!" Birch slowly settled down and took his seat behind the table. "Let it be made known throughout the regiment that no one is to speak of what happened or they will get the lash. In my report I will state that we were ambushed. I don't want word getting out that we were bested and humiliated by a colonist."

Loftus, thinking the interview was over, saluted and turned to leave. Birch, speaking more sympathetically, said, "Lieutenant Loftus, I know who that man was. I recall his blue sash and the very high quality of the tailoring on his uniform. After interrogating prisoners we learned it was none other than the Rebel commander, George Washington. The blue sash designates that. Do not worry. The rebellion is nearly crushed. The residents of this city treat us as heroes. I'm sure most of the Colonists are loyal to the king. It's only these few rabble rousers. Mark my words. You and I will see this Washington hang by Christmas."

CHAPTER TEN

Rangers

Washington's Headquarters, Morris House, Harlem Heights,
September 16th, 1776, 5:30 A.M.

WASHINGTON WAS AT his desk, going over correspondence and preparing the orders of the day by candlelight. Sunrise would not come for another hour. There was a knock at the door. Without looking up, Washington replied, "Enter."

Lieutenant Colonel Thomas Knowlton opened the door and came forward to Washington's desk. "Reporting as ordered, General."

Washington responded, "Lieutenant Colonel Knowlton, I have an important assignment for you this very morning. I want you to ascertain the precise location of the enemy lines and troop dispositions. In addition, I must know if they are planning an attack this day. I am counting on your Rangers to perform this important reconnaissance. Do not fire unless fired upon. I do not desire a general engagement at this time. When will you be able to depart?"

"We can depart immediately, General," Knowlton replied.

Washington shared one of his rare smiles, "Very good. I have the utmost confidence in you and your men."

"By your leave sir," Knowlton said, as he saluted and turned to leave.

Washington had the greatest respect for Knowlton. He had used him and his Rangers extensively during the siege of Boston to gather information on the enemy. The Rangers also performed many night raids against the British. One raid in particular was both bold and humorous at the same time. It was one of the more memorable escapades of the Revolution.

The British in Boston were desperate for firewood. They had taken to pulling down abandoned houses to use the wood for fuel that winter. To deprive them of this resource, Knowlton led a detachment of 200 men to set fire to the 14 remaining houses in Charlestown. This area was under the guns of the formidable British fortifications on Bunker's Hill. Knowlton and his men set out at 8 P.M. on January 8, 1776. As the raiders went to work torching the houses, the guns opened up at the British fortification nearby. They fired in confusion, in all directions, not knowing exactly where the Rangers were. It just so happened that it was opening night for the play "The Blockade of Boston," written by General John Burgoyne. The play was being performed in Faneuil Hall by British officers. At the moment an actor stepped onto the stage, mocking General Washington, another member of the cast came running on stage and yelled, "The Yankees are attacking our works on Bunker's Hill!" The audience laughed uproariously, thinking it was part of the play.

"But soon finding their mistake [wrote an eye witness], a general scene of confusion ensued. They immediately hurried out of the house to their alarm posts, some skipping over the orchestra, trampling on the fiddles, and, in short, everyone making a speedy retreat, the actors (who were all officers) calling for water to get the paint and smut off their faces, women fainting, etc."

That morning, as Knowlton left Washington's headquarters, heading directly to his men, it struck him that Washington had the kindest look in his eyes he had ever seen. As was typical of Knowlton, before meeting with Washington he had shown initiative in leaving orders to have the men ready to march as soon as possible. He had assumed he was called to meet with Washington to do reconnaissance.

"Fall in," Knowlton ordered. The Rangers formed two ranks, facing Knowlton. "We are to perform reconnaissance of the enemy lines. We shall do this without being observed, if possible. We will fire only if fired upon. Once we march out of camp I will be giving orders quietly, so as not to be detected by the enemy. Watch the man to your right and pay close attention. Once we enter the Hollow Way* we shall display in the extended order at 5-pace intervals. The second section will break off. As we will be in one long line, this will give us the greatest opportunity to take note of any enemy positions." Knowlton took his place at the head of the column and gave the commands, "Left face! At the rout step, to the front march!" The detachment of 120 Rangers left the Patriot camp and disappeared into the early morning darkness. By the end of the day they would be fewer in number.

Justus Bellamy, who was getting the fire started for his mess,† watched as the Rangers left camp. His mess mates had gathered around the fire and watched also. Bellamy shared, "It appears that Knowlton and his Rangers are heading out looking for Redcoats. I have spoken with one of the fellows in his regiment. He told me that Knowlton would never say 'Go on boys,' it is always 'Come on boys.' He always goes first into danger, and his men follow."

Just as the Rangers left a wood and entered the Hollow Way, Knowlton gave the command to display in the extended order. The 120 Rangers then walked forward in one long line at 5-pace intervals. As the commander, Knowlton was at the right end of

---

* Hollow Way: A flat open area free of trees between the Patriot and British lines. The Patriots were encamped at Harlem Heights, today known as Morningside Heights. There were some small rolling hills beyond the Hollow Way. The British were just beyond those hills.
† The "mess" was the smallest unit in an 18th-century army, usually consisting of 6 men. They would share the same tent and cook their meals together.

the Rangers, closest to the North River. A horseman approached from their rear. It was one of Washington's aides-de-camp, Lieutenant Colonel Joseph Reed. Reed approached Knowlton and said quietly, "I am here to observe and to get word back quickly to the General should the need arise."

Knowlton replied at a whisper, "Very well, but keep to our rear by 25 paces." As they got just beyond the halfway mark of the Hollow Way, a fence line entangled with bushes was encountered. The Rangers climbed over. Knowlton found a fence section with the least amount of brush and had two men remove fence poles to make a path for Reed's horse.

The Rangers completed their crossing of the Hollow Way, encountering another fence entangled with brush, and now entered a wood and began ascending Claremont Hill.* Knowlton looked over his right shoulder at the summit and got a clear view of the North River. As they continued downhill they came across a low stone wall. The area was still heavily wooded. Knowlton sent word down the line that this stone wall on the hill was to be a "rally point." In case the Rangers needed to withdraw in a hurry, they would meet up at that spot by the stone wall. It was almost dawn. As the Rangers continued on they entered a large buckwheat field. They crossed the field and entered another wood. Knowlton saw a farmhouse to his right, through a clearing. Having spoken with some men local to the area, he knew it to be the Hogeland Farmhouse. He was also told that the Jones Farmhouse was less than a quarter mile from the Hogeland Farmhouse, down the Bloomingdale Road. The Rangers then entered an orchard. At the end of the orchard there was a small cross-road connecting the Bloomingdale and Old Post Roads. Knowlton could see the intersection with the Bloomingdale Road, not more than a stone's throw away. Surprisingly, there was still no sign of the Redcoats.

---

* Claremont Hill is the present-day location of Grant's Tomb.

Private Percival Tavington of the British light infantry was on advanced picket duty.* He was disgusted. He could have been back with his messmates eating breakfast. Instead, it was his turn for picket duty. To guard against what, he thought to himself, an attack from the cowardly Rebels? All the Rebels did was to run away. Show them the bayonet and off they go. They wouldn't even stand and fight, let alone attack. It was 6:40 A.M. The rays of the sun started to penetrate past the tree line. As the morning light illuminated the area around him, he saw movement in the distance to the north. Thinking his eyes were deceiving him, he rubbed them with his hand. It can't be, he thought to himself. He saw a long line of more than 100 men coming toward him. Rebels advancing? He hesitated for a moment; there must be some mistake. As incredulous as it was, he had to do his duty. He took aim with his musket, fired at the Rebels, and yelled back over his shoulder at the top of his lungs, "TO ARMS, TO ARMS!"

---

* See the end note in reference to page 19, "four elite battalions," for a review of the makeup of a British infantry regiment.

CHAPTER ELEVEN

The Foxhunting Horn at Harlem Heights

The British Army Frontline, Mid-Manhattan, September 16th, 6:40 A.M.

TAVINGTON DETESTED THE idea of showing his back to the lowly Rebels. But he had to report back. As he turned and ran back toward the Jones Farmhouse it occurred to him that something far worse awaited him, the laughter of his fellow soldiers. His shot most likely caused the Rebels to run away. Now no one would believe that he had seen anything. He had to clear a 4-foot fence to get back to the British lines. Tavington was a short man, but nimble. Stepping up on the middle fence pole, he quickly gained the top pole, jumped to the ground, and ran to the Jones Farmhouse.

Knowlton, meanwhile, signaled a stop by raising his hand. He spoke quickly and quietly to the man to his left, Lieutenant Abner Bacon. "Abner, send word quietly down the line to bring the men up to the fence and take cover behind it. The second section of 60 is to take position behind the first rank. Maintain the 5-pace intervals. Have them prime and load [they had been unloaded up to this point to prevent an accidental discharge, which would have revealed their presence]. I am going over the fence to get a closer look at their encampment. March-March."

Bacon ran down the line quietly issuing the orders. Knowlton was 6-foot tall, lean, and agile. The fence line was very much like the one in the Hollow Way. Brush was growing through it. He ran for the fence, and switching his musket to his left hand, reached out with his right, grabbed the upper fence pole, and vaulted over in a single movement. Landing lightly on his feet, he made for a clump of brush near a tree, a stone's throw from the Jones Farmhouse. Upon arrival, he got down on one knee to get a look at the camp.

Private Tavington didn't look back. Never in his wildest dreams would he consider the possibility of being followed by the Rebels. All was activity in the camp. The drummers were beating the "To Arms" order. The troops were gathering their cartridge boxes and muskets. All of this noise drowned out what little noise the Rangers were making. Tavington ran up to his sergeant, saluted, and gave his report. Sergeant Lionel Hobbs looked to the north and saw nothing. Hobbs replied, "Tavington, did you get into some rum at the Hogeland Farmhouse?" Tavington's worst fears were being realized. He would be a laughing stock.

"No, Sergeant," Tavington replied, "I never left my post. I fired my alarm shot at 'em. The Rebels must've run off like they do." Sergeant Hobbs's expression turned more serious. He knew Tavington was not prone to wild exaggeration.

"Come with me Tavington," said Hobbs. "We shall report to Captain Prentiss. You will tell him exactly what you told me."

Meanwhile, Lieutenant Abner Bacon was back in his position to the right of the first section, facing the enemy. The second section was right behind. All muskets were loaded. All the Rangers were crouching on one knee behind the fence entangled with bushes. Sergeant David Thorp, who was to the left of Bacon, whispered, "Lieutenant, what's the commander about to do? Is he going to take on the whole British Army by himself?"

"The man has no fear," Bacon replied.

Knowlton had heard the whole conversation between the enemy private and sergeant. He was able to take in the whole camp. All light infantry, except the 42nd Highlanders and a regiment of

Hessians, mercenaries from Germany.* He saw what he had come to see. As the sergeant and private turned and walked away, he saw his opportunity. Knowlton turned around and trotted back to the fence. He went unnoticed by the British.

Knowlton considered his options. He had accomplished his objective: he had found the enemy's forward-most position and had ascertained troop strength. General Washington had ordered, "Do not fire unless fired upon. I do not desire a general engagement at this time." They had been observed by the Redcoats, so the Rangers' presence was no longer a secret. The enemy was getting into battle formation to pursue. If he left the fence now, the Rangers would surely be observed in the open ground between the fence and the wood. He was in an ideal position to ambush the Redcoats. Being of an aggressive nature, Knowlton decided to stand and fight.

The 2nd and 3rd Light Infantry Battalions were lined up in formation, ready to move out. Also ready were troops from the 42nd Regiment—that is, the Royal Highland Regiment, the Black Watch, known as one of the toughest regiments in the British Army. During the Seven Years' War, 1756–1763, the Black Watch took part in the attack on what was to become known as Fort Ticonderoga. It was built by the French and originally named Fort Carillion. In 1758, the Black Watch took part in several furious frontal assaults against the French outer fortifications, taking terrible casualties and yet refusing to give up.

Having been briefed by Sergeant Hobbs, Captain Arthur Prentiss reported to Brigadier General Alexander Leslie, the commander of all light troops. General Leslie was at breakfast with his staff. Prentiss saluted and gave the report. Leslie replied, "I believe the young private was seeing things. However, in the remote chance it is proven to be true, it would be prudent to send out a reconnaissance in force. The effort will not be wasted. I would like to know if the Rebels are even still on the island. "Colonel Hamond,"

---

* See the end notes for more on Highlanders and Hessians.

Leslie continued, "take out several companies of light infantry and the 42nd. Hold the Jaegers* as a reserve. They could be useful should you make contact. Those fellows are at home in the woodlands."

Colonel Ashley Hamond had some 400 men under his command. All elite troops. It was now 7:30 A.M. He gave the order and the troops moved out. The 42nd held the center, with the lights on each flank, from the 2nd and 3rd Battalions. The Jaegers were ordered to be ready to march at a moment's notice. Hamond thought they would be unnecessary. This whole exercise was a waste of effort except for the chance of finding out whether the Rebels had left the island. Even if the enemy were encountered, they could push back the whole Rebel Army with these 400 men. The mere sight of a few light infantry had sent hundreds of Rebels to flight the day before. Hamond went on to think that if this reconnaissance in force went well, it could mean a promotion for him.

The first obstacle was a fence line entangled with brush. When the British got within 50 yards, they were shocked to hear a stout command from the other side, "STAND." The other commands followed quickly, "Cock your firelocks, Present, FIRE!" All 120 Rangers fired their muskets. The rear rank fired over the shoulders of the first rank. Several of the Redcoats went down. Hamond was dumbfounded. This was completely unexpected. No sooner had the volley ripped into the British ranks than the Rebel commander yelled, "Let them see that we can stand and fight! Panics don't last overnight!" All the Rangers cheered in unison, "HUZZA!"

General Leslie heard the musketry and the huzza, and choked on his tea. As soon as he could clear his throat he ordered for his spyglass. There was a farm wagon nearby, and he climbed atop it. Looking through his spyglass, he exclaimed, "It must be those blasted Rangers! They gave us a devil of a time in Boston! Get

---

* Jaegers were Hessian light troops specifically chosen from men who were trained hunters and were familiar with the woods.

word to Colonel Hamond to flank them and annihilate them! I have had enough of those Rangers!"

After one mass volley, Knowlton started firing by rank. This way, one rank out of two was always loaded and ready to fire in case they were rushed. The benefit of the extended order, his men at 5-pace intervals, was that they would present a much longer front than if in a tight shoulder-to-shoulder formation. The Rangers were much more difficult to flank* in this extended order.

Knowlton had fired six volleys per rank when he noticed an ominous change in the Redcoat formation. The 42nd Highlanders stepped forward 5 paces, went to the extended order, and fired. As they had in essence stepped in front of the light infantry, and with the smoke of their volley now hanging in the air, the light infantry on either side of the Highlanders were hidden from view. Knowlton immediately grasped the purpose of the movement. It was a screen. The light infantry had been sent out to flank them. Bravery under fire was one thing, suicide was another. The Rangers were outnumbered almost 4 to 1. Knowlton also had to get back to Washington with his intelligence.

Knowlton gave the order to withdraw, "First rank, withdraw 50 paces, second rank, withdraw 25 paces! Maintain the extended order! March-March!" As soon as the first rank was in position at 25 paces he gave the order to fire and retire 50 paces. Each of the two ranks provided cover for the other as the whole unit withdrew. This was not a retreat in a panic, but an orderly withdrawal. The Rangers had taken some casualties, but they could walk. Each Ranger had fired eight rounds. Knowlton could see that the Highlanders had charged the fence and were climbing over. Now was the time, "To the Rally Point!" All the Rangers knew it was time to move with all haste to Claremont Hill.

Knowlton approached Reed, "Lieutenant Colonel Reed, I would

---

* The danger in any battle is to be "flanked," wherein an enemy gets around the ends of the firing line and has the ability to hit from behind or the unprotected sides.

be greatly obliged if you were to inform General Washington of our predicament." Reed replied, "Most certainly Lieutenant Colonel Knowlton. I shall do so immediately." Reed turned his horse and cantered off.

The Rangers made it back to the rally point at Claremont Hill, having passed through the orchard, the wood, and buckwheat field without taking any casualties. Knowlton got the men in position behind the low stone wall. They were loaded and ready to fire. The walking wounded, and those with other, more serious wounds from the initial encounter at the British lines, came limping into the rally point, assisted by their brothers in arms. "Step lively, Boys! As quick as you can!" Knowlton commanded. "We will hold them till you are able to get back to our lines." The Redcoats were right on their heels. As the last of the wounded cleared the Ranger line, Knowlton gave the firing commands, "First rank, cock firelocks, present, FIRE!"

The light infantry and Highlanders had lost unit cohesion during the chase. They took several minutes to reform and redeploy to return fire. This was the delay Knowlton wanted, a chance to get his wounded back behind the Patriot lines. He knew that if left behind, they probably would be bayoneted. Knowlton continued, "First rank, prime and load. Second rank, cock firelocks, present, FIRE!" Knowlton's motive now was to delay the Redcoats and prevent more casualties. "First rank, withdraw 25 paces. Second rank, withdraw 50 paces and prime and load!" The Rangers had completed the movement before the British had a chance to fire. By the time the Redcoats returned fire it was ineffective. Claremont Hill was heavily wooded and had an ample amount of brush. The light infantry and Highlanders continued their pursuit.

Knowlton completed two more fire-and-retire movements and found himself near the foot of the hill. The woods were coming to an end. The Hollow Way was before them. He ordered the Rangers to climb over the fence just beyond the bottom of the hill. Seeing his wounded men were nearing the fence deeper into the Hollow Way, which they had climbed over earlier, Knowlton commanded, "To the next fence! March-March!" Seeing the Rangers making for the fence across the Hollow Way, the British light infantry were content to stop and watch from the top of Claremont Hill. The British light troops had been keeping up what for the moment seemed to them a merry chase. Tavington caught his breath along with the others. He had gathered with the men from his mess and exclaimed, "You see, I was right, I was not out of my head. There were Rebels."

Private Braddock commented, "We see that now as plain as day, Tavington. What we want to know is why you didn't chase them yourself from the start and save us all the trouble!" All the men in Tavington's mess laughed heartily, except Tavington.

Washington was at the most forward position of the Patriot lines. He was accompanied by Billy Lee and another aide-de-camp, Lieutenant Colonel Tench Tilghman. Washington was mounted on Blueskin. Nelson needed some well-earned rest after the exertions of the day before. Washington had heard all the musketry coming toward the Patriot lines. He was troubled as to why he had not been informed of the action. Reed cantered up to him and saluted, "General, the Rangers have put up a fine fight against the enemy. They stood their ground for several volleys before being overwhelmed by superior numbers."

Washington replied, "That is commendable, all well and good. However, I did not want a general engagement this day. After the drubbing we took yesterday the men are not ready."

The Redcoats viewed the Rebel retreat with eyes of contempt. Sergeant Hobbs commented, "It's a fine day for another chase. Not unlike a fox hunt, dealing with these Rebels. Well, that's a thought. Bring up the bugler. There's a good fellow, now play the fox hunt call. We shall have a little fun with those rascals." The bugler played and the hill was filled with laughter. Hobbs continued, "Come on fellows, let them also hear our light infantry song." The light troops near Hobbs shared the refrain:

Hark! Hark! The bugle's lofty sound
Which makes the woods and rocks around
Repeat the martial strain,

Proclaims the light-armed British troops
Advance—Behold, rebellion droops,
She hears the sound with pain.

The sound of the fox-hunt call was clearly heard throughout the Patriot lines. All understood the severity of the insult. Reed shared with the small group around Washington, "I never felt such a sensation before—it seemed to crown our disgrace." An avid foxhunter, Washington was particularly stung by it. Billy Lee, Reed, and Tilghman eyed Washington. Through a lifetime of training, Washington had taught himself to control his emotions. He did have a temper. Even though he was able to control it most of the time, men could sense it. Part of his mystique as a leader and the strong image he personified came from this. Men could sense this unseen power. Washington began formulating a plan in his mind. He recalled his thoughts of the day before. Here was an opportunity to use the enemy's contempt as a weapon against it.

Back on Claremont Hill, Captain Prentiss did not join in with the laughter. These Rebels were not the same as the ones they had chased so easily the day before. These men had backbone. They stood and fought and withdrew in good order when in danger of being flanked. He and the other officers congregated around Colonel Hamond, who was observing the Rebel lines through his spyglass. Although the Rebel positions were partly obscured by the woods on the opposite side of the Hollow Way, Hamond could make out some of the Rebel troops in the distance. It was now 9 A.M. Hamond addressed the officers, "We shall remain here and establish a new forward position to launch our next assault. Have a runner sent back and give a report to General Leslie. We shall have the Jaegers brought up to explore our right flank." The orders were written by a lieutenant, who sent a runner back to the advanced camp of the Crown forces. Hamond thought to himself that this opportunity could be the pathway to promotion to brigadier.

CHAPTER TWELVE

The Trap Is Set

The Continental Army Front Line, Harlem Heights,
September 16th, 9 A.M.

KNOWLTON ARRIVED AND reported to Washington, "General, there are some 400 light troops on Claremont Hill. I did see a regiment of Hessians that included Jaegers at the enemy's encampment. They remained behind. What we ran into at the Jones Farmhouse was the advanced position of the light infantry. The main army was some distance to the south."

Washington addressed him, "Lieutenant Colonel Knowlton, you must have gotten very close to them to obtain that information. Are you prepared to return to the field presently?"

"That I am sir!" Knowlton replied.

Washington went on, "These Ministerialists are arrogant fellows. They hold our marshal spirit in complete contempt. We shall use that as a weapon against them. I want you to get to their rear and attack them from behind. We shall lure them into the Hollow Way with a demonstration to their front and feign a retreat. I wager that it is a bet we cannot lose that they will come forward into the Hollow Way. You shall push them from behind. I will send another regiment to reinforce you. Get your Rangers into position to the far left of our lines. At the sound of musketry make your move. Lieutenant Colonel Reed will join you with the reinforcements shortly." Knowlton saluted and ran off to his men.

Washington gave orders to his aides-de-camp in quick succession. "Mr. Reed, here is an opportunity for our army to recover its military ardor, which is of the utmost moment to an army. Ride post-haste to Colonel Weedon's 3rd Virginia Regiment. Have Major Andrew Leitch join his regiment with Lieutenant Colonel Knowlton's immediately. I know all the officers from this regiment. They are from the Fredericksburg area—brave stalwart fellows all. They will not let the Rangers down. Go!" Reed spurred his horse and took off at the gallop. Washington turned to Tilghman. "Mr. Tilghman, gather your fellow Marylanders with the Flying Camp.* They are to act as a reserve, ready to support Knowlton and Leitch. Go!" Tilghman in turn galloped off. Washington and Billy Lee rode off at full gallop in another direction. Lee was so in tune with Washington that he did not need to be told. He just knew to stay by Washington's side.

The Abbot brothers were encamped near a 4-foot fence. They were part of Nixon's brigade. Asa said to his brother James, "Look there! General Washington is approaching with great speed!" Washington and Will jumped the fence in unison and landed simultaneously within 20 feet of the Abbots. The brothers' mouths hung open as they watched the jump. James exclaimed to Asa, "I have never seen such fine horsemen as these two!" The brothers watched as Washington and his servant approached the command tent of the recently promoted Brigadier General John Nixon.

Washington and Lee came to a sliding stop just short of Nixon and his staff. Nixon, a bit taken aback by the dramatic entrance, paused for a moment until he remembered to salute. Washington returned the salute and gave orders to Lee, "Will, go fetch General Greene!" Billy Lee was off in the blink of an eye and soon disappeared from view. Nixon's brigade was under the command of Major General Nathanael Greene.

---

* Flying Camp explained in end notes.

Washington turned his attention to Nixon. "General Nixon, the game is afoot. We have the opportunity to bag a group of enemy light infantry who are over extended. We shall entrap them. Select 100 men or more to march forward as a feint to the Hollow Way. They shall engage the light infantry on Claremont Hill. Have them take position on the fence line and fire. This will most assuredly draw in the enemy to pursue. The feint party will retire at the run to the wood on our side of the Hollow Way. You will be hidden there with your entire brigade in support. As soon as the feint party is safely behind you, open fire. Do not advance, but keep them engaged in place. We are to have another force moving to their rear. You must wait to advance until they are in place. Bring up two cannon. Do not use them until the trap is set. Then rake them with grape shot. Prepare to move out immediately. No drums. If you beat to arms we may be heard by the enemy. Fix bayonets before you leave the encampment for the same reason. Is this understood?" Once again taken aback, Nixon paused. He could see the look of steel in Washington's eyes.

"Yes your Excellency," he finally replied, "we shall set the plan into motion this instant!"

At that moment Lee arrived with General Greene, and Washington addressed Greene: "General Greene, ride with me. I have much to explain."

Lieutenant Colonel Archibald Crary of Hitchcock's Rhode Island Regiment led 150 of his men out to the Hollow Way. This was the feint party to draw out the enemy. Nixon's entire brigade, some 900 strong, took position in a heavily wooded area on the edge of the hollow way. Two 6-pound cannons were wheeled into place. This was all done out of view from the Redcoats. Soldiers climbed trees to keep an eye on the enemy's movements. The Abbot brothers were part of Nixon's brigade. They were stationed on the right flank, close to the North River. Sergeant Bellamy and his men were on the extreme left flank, closer to the East River. All were itching for a fight after yesterday's debacle.

Back on Claremont Hill, Colonel Hamond was discussing strategy with other officers when he was interrupted by a lieutenant, "Sir, I beg your pardon, but Rebels are approaching." Incredulous, Hamond spun around and looked for himself, "Rebels advancing! Astonishing! We cannot bear to be insulted by these upstarts! Prepare to attack!" Crary had lined up his men on the same fence line (just beyond the halfway mark in the Hollow Way) that the Rangers had climbed over earlier. On the Patriot side of the fence, Crary opened fire on the Redcoats. It was 10 A.M. The battle of Harlem Heights had begun.

The Hessian Jaegers had just arrived, with Captain Von Wreden in command. He had 50 men in total divided into two platoons, one platoon of musketeers from a Grenadier company to support the one platoon of Jaeger riflemen. Hamond positioned them on his right flank, closer to the East River. They were to act as a reserve and stay behind the woodline, out of view of the Rebels. They would be protecting the Redcoats' right flank. The light infantry charged down the hill with fixed bayonets. They came down diagonally, heading northeast. They delighted in the bayonets, as they knew the Rebels had such fear of them. Crary was able to get off three volleys before withdrawing. Several Redcoats were hit. As Crary and his men ran to the wood line on the Patriot side of the Hollow Way, Nixon brought his whole brigade out of the woods. The two cannon were left hidden for the moment. Crary and his men took their position on the right flank, next to the Abbot brothers' company. Nixon gave the command, "Brigade volley! Cock your firelocks! Present! FIRE!" Nine hundred muskets let loose a fearsome boom and a burst of smoke. The Redcoats had just taken up position on the fence line. They in turn fired a volley.

As Washington watched from the woods, he commented to General Greene, "All is going perfectly according to plan. At this moment Knowlton and Leitch are on their way."

While the firing was furious in the Hollow Way, Knowlton, Leitch, and their men made their way south from the extreme left of the Patriot lines, not far from the Harlem River. They were joined by Reed on horseback. The Maryland Flying Camp brought up the rear, accompanied by Tench Tilghman on horseback. It was 10:45 A.M.

A junior officer in the 3rd Virginia Regiment was well ahead of the column, acting as a scout. He began directing the men to turn west, toward the Redcoats. Reed was troubled. They were heading west too soon. He rode over and addressed the junior officer, "You are turning too soon. We must go farther south." In reply the junior officer stated, "When we clear the rocky outcrop ahead, we shall be in line with Claremont Hill." By this time both regiments were streaming toward the rocky hill. Reed realized it was too late to change course now.

It was now nearing 11:00 A.M. Hamond was dismayed. What had begun as a merry chase had turned into a bloody affair. He was outnumbered 2 to 1. The numbers were starting to tell. He then saw two cannon emerge from the Rebel lines. The command was given, "Withdraw!" The Redcoats fell back and reformed just east of the foot of Claremont Hill, behind the other fence. Nixon gave the command, "Brigade, to the front, March-March!" As the Redcoats reformed at the foot of the hill, Nixon's Brigade seized the vacated fence line. The opposing forces were now approximately 200 paces apart, both behind fence lines entangled with brush. Nixon ordered another Brigade volley. Simultaneously, Knowlton and Leitch appeared at the top of the rocky outcrop. The hill had kept them completely hidden from the British. Knowlton and Leitch grasped their mistake. They were attacking the flank. They had not gone far enough to the rear of the enemy. It was too late now. They had to attack. Knowlton commanded his men, "Come on, boys!"

The Hessians, on the extreme British right, had been out of the fight—as ordered—until now. They saw the movement on top of the rocky outcrop. Knowlton and Leitch led their men down the slope and halted just beyond the summit. The Redcoats were 60 yards away. The Hessians remained unseen in the woods. Knowlton and Leitch gave the command to fire into the British flank. Tench Tilghman, some distance back with the Marylanders, perceived what had happened, hearing the firing ahead. Tilghman conferred with the officers of the Flying Camp, "Gentlemen, it is plain the plan to attack in the rear has gone awry. Let us take this opportunity to get further behind their flank." All concurred, and the movement was begun at March-March. A runner was sent west to inform Knowlton and Leitch. The Marylanders headed due south into the wood. As the soldiers of the Flying Camp made their way into the woods, they were observed by a group of four Jaeger pickets. They had been well placed, some distance away from the main body of Jaegers, to protect the rear. Realizing the danger, the four Jaegers pickets melted away under cover and returned quickly to the main body.

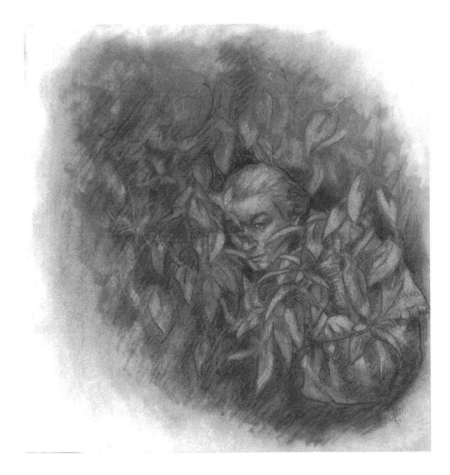

CHAPTER THIRTEEN

Heroes Fall

The Hollow Way, September 16th, 11:00 A.M.

CAPTAIN WREDEN OF the Jaegers ordered his musketeer platoon to step out of the woods and volley fire. Leitch was hit twice in the stomach, he staggered but remained on his feet. Other men close by him fell. The Hessians were at a right angle [as in an "L"] to their British counterparts, but there was a 30-yard gap. Seeing both Rebel officers still standing, Wreden stepped forward 20 paces by himself to get a better shot and targeted one of the senior officers. He had not fired his rifled musket* in the volley. Wreden took aim and fired.

Knowlton, leading from the front as always, got hit and dropped to the ground. The ball had entered the small of his back. The shot had come from a direction perpendicular to him. He fell within a few feet of Captain Stephen Brown of the Rangers. Brown was quickly by his side and propped him up and asked, "Are you

---

* A rifled musket had grooves cut in the barrel in a spiral. This put a spin on the bullet, making it much more accurate than the typical smoothbore musket.

badly wounded?" Knowlton replied, "I do not value my life if we but get the day. By all means, keep up this flank attack." Brown ordered two Rangers to get Knowlton back to their lines. As Knowlton was carried away, Brown was struck by his demeanor. Knowlton seemed as unconcerned and calm as though nothing had happened to him.

During this pause, Wreden returned to his original position with his men. At that moment, he was approached by one of the pickets, "Herr Hauptman, ein Trupp Rebellen bewegt sich hinter uns! [Captain, a Rebel force is moving behind us!]" Wreden ordered a withdrawal to link up with the British.

Nixon, seeing action between the Rangers and the suddenly appearing Hessians, gave orders for a third of his brigade to move forward in support. The remaining two thirds kept up a galling fire on the British. Troops on the Patriot left advanced. Bellamy's company was on the extreme left.

The Rangers were to the left of the Virginians. Brown took command and approached Leitch, "Major, we should take to the woods after those Hessians and keep pressure on the enemy's flank. Nixon is sending more men to help. Are you hit sir? You don't look well."

Leitch replied, "I am still able to command. What you suggest is correct. We shall do so presently." At that instant another Jaeger sharpshooter found his mark. Leitch was hit in the hip, his pelvis shattered. He fell to the ground instantly. Captain William Washington and Lieutenant James Monroe came to his side.[*] Leitch spoke to Washington: "Captain, take command." After ordering two men to take Leitch to the rear, Captain Washington ordered his men into the woods along with the Rangers. Thanks to the message from the runner sent by Tilghman, the Rangers and Virginians were aware of the presence of the Marylanders deeper into the woods.

---

[*] William Washington, a distant cousin of the commander, was present in the 3rd Virginia Regiment at the battle, along with James Monroe, who went on to become the 5th president of the United States.

The Hessians fell back, firing and retiring as they went. They now faced a new threat. Rebels from across the Hollow Way were bearing down on them. They formed themselves into their own "L" formation, with Rebels on their right and their front. Wreden gave command of the small force to a lieutenant and ran to the British. They must be informed of the new threat in the rear. Wreden saw Captain Prentiss in the distance and ran toward him. Communication between the Germans and British was often difficult. Wreden and Prentiss both knew French. They had discovered they spoke a common language the day before. Wreden addressed Prentiss, "Mon Capitaine, une Force Rebelle se deplace derriere Vous." [Captain, a Rebel force is moving behind us.] Prentiss replied, "Je vais avertir le Colonel immediatement." [I shall warn the Colonel immediately.] Wreden returned to his men.

At the moment that Prentiss had finished explaining the new threat to Hamond, two cannons fired in quick succession from the Rebel lines. Hamond spoke his mind out loud, "Cannon to our front, a flank attack to our right, Rebels encircling us in our rear through the wood, this cannot be happening! We need to reform in the buckwheat field. Let them come and fight us in the open instead of skulking about in the wood, as they are so fond. They will not be able to stand and fight in the open in proper European fashion! Lieutenant Aubrey, make all due haste and return to our lines. Have our remaining light infantry and Grenadiers, and the Hessian Grenadiers, brought up to the buckwheat field immediately! And bring up some cannon! We shall give them a fight!"

Instead of returning over Claremont Hill and through the woods, as they had come, Hamond brought his force through open ground directly to the buckwheat field. Nixon ordered his brigade forward and quickly took the fence line abandoned by the Redcoats. As the Black Watch withdrew, they were beside themselves. The Scotsmen spoke to themselves in Gaelic, wondering why they were retreating when they should be on the attack.

Washington, observing the attack with pride, spoke to Greene, "The attack from the rear has not gone as planned. However, the assault is progressing admirably. Let us not lose this opportunity. Bring up the rest of your division in support. Attack from our left, drive the enemy back." "Very good sir, it will be done post-haste!" Greene replied. Washington addressed Billy Lee, "Will, be a good fellow and fetch General Putnam for me."

General Leslie was concerned. He heard musketry getting closer. Leslie spoke with his staff, including Captain John Montresor. "What is happening?" Leslie demanded. "What is Colonel Hamond about? I should be informed!" At that moment, Lieutenant Aubrey, who had been sent by Hamond, arrived. The lieutenant saluted, "General Leslie, Colonel Hamond has request-ed that the remaining light infantry, our grenadiers, and the Hessian Grenadiers be sent in support, as well as some cannon. The Rebels are attacking in strength, and we have been forced to withdraw and take up a new position in the buckwheat field."

"What?" Leslie replied. "That is ridiculous! Colonel Hamond has some of the finest troops in our army! How can he be with-drawing from those pitiful Rebels!" Leslie paced around for a few moments to collect his thoughts and then addressed his staff. "Our grenadiers are some distance away, near the city. Send a rider at once to have them brought forward. The Hessian Grenadiers are closer at hand; get them in place at once. Captain Montresor, see to it that at least two cannon are brought forward. Lieutenant Blair, have my horse saddled for me. I must report to General Howe."

Meanwhile, Bellamy and his company had gotten ahead of all the other units in the Continentals' oblique advance. They were about to link up with the Virginians. Bellamy saw a Hessian take a hit and fall. One of his Hessian comrades stopped to help him. Bellamy had an instant flashback to the Battle of Long Island ear-lier that summer.

He had been with his company, in a desperate situation; they were about to be overrun and cut off by the Hessians. Seeing no officers in sight, and as the only leader present, Bellamy had to make a decision. Bellamy gave the final command to fire; he knew the smoke would help hide their movements. "Quickly lads, make for the fortifications at Brooklyn, every man for himself! Run for your lives!" They had no sooner turned around and started to run when Bellamy's childhood friend, Thomas Baines, took a hit in the leg and collapsed.

Bellamy stopped to help his friend. Baines said, "Justus, you must leave me and go on. The men of our company cannot do without you." Bellamy replied, "I can't just leave you here. Come on, Thomas, put your arm over my shoulder and I will help you." Baines continued, "Justus, you must leave me now, they are almost on top of us. I will be taken prisoner and will be fine. I cannot bear to have us both captured. The men need you. Go!"

Bellamy sprinted off. Within 40 yards he came to a stone wall and jumped over it. He kneeled down to hide himself and peered over the wall to witness the fate of his dear friend. Baines, sitting on the ground, put his hands up in surrender as the Hessians approached. Three of them came right up to Baines and bayoneted him, each in turn. Bellamy turned away and banged on the ground with his hand in a fist. "No, no, what have I done!" He said to himself. He looked over once again. Two Hessians stood up Baines's limp body and held him against a tree. A third man drove Baines's own bayonet through his body, pinning him to the tree. He used Baines's musket butt as a hammer. Bellamy was stunned. He had never seen such cruelty. He finally came to his senses and sprinted off. He did not want the same fate to befall him.

As the flashback brought this terrible memory to Bellamy, he snapped. Bellamy broke from the ranks and ran full tilt with his bayonet at the Hessian who was helping his comrade. The Hessian, who had been keeping a wary eye as he tried to get his comrade to safety, set his comrade down and prepared for the attack. The man coming at him looked like a crazed maniac. An eight-year veteran of many campaigns in Europe, he was not worried. He would use the man's own insanity as a weapon against him. He would remain cool-headed and take advantage of an angry beginner's mistake. He had performed countless bayonet drills in practice. What could this Rebel do to him, a professional?

Bellamy was always the master of the unorthodox. He seldom did what others expected. Not only was he athletic, but he was a powerful man. As Bellamy closed in on the Hessian, he let go of his musket with his left hand and reached forward and grabbed the Hessian's musket where the bayonet attached to the muzzle. Still holding his own musket with an iron grip in his right hand, Bellamy slammed the musket stock into the face of the Hessian with a powerful blow. With the force of the blow and the weight of Bellamy's body, and all the momentum behind it, the Hessian fell backward. Instinctively, the Hessian let go of his musket with his right hand, still clutching the barrel end with his left, and reached behind to break the fall. On impact, Bellamy set his own musket down, tore the Hessian's musket out of his hand, and threw it aside. Bellamy then grabbed the Hessian by the shirt collar and repeatedly punched him in the head with the force of a blacksmith's hammer. After several blows Bellamy began to strangle him and yelled, "You Hessian bastards! You butchered Thomas! I'm going to pin your friend to a tree, just as you did to Thomas!" All the while, the Hessian's wounded comrade had been crawling over to help. With every ounce of strength he had, the wounded Hessian raised his bayonet and prepared to thrust it into the crazed Rebel.

On the extreme right flank of the Patriot lines, the Abbot brothers were in a furious firefight with the retreating Redcoats. Captain Chamberlain was giving the orders to his company, "Cock your firelocks! Present! FIRE!" Flame and smoke burst forth from the muskets in the Abbot brothers' company. Down the Patriot line similar discharges took place and found their mark. Redcoat casualties were mounting. The Continentals were also taking hits. Colonel Hamond kept his withdrawal in motion through the buckwheat field, firing and retiring. He gave orders to the unit commanders, "Form a line here! We will stop those Rebels cold! Here is some fine open ground! They won't have their precious trees, bushes, and walls to hide behind! They cannot stand and fight in the open!"

Nixon gave his brigade the command to advance, "Brigade! To the Front! March!" The drummers by his side beat out the commands. In the din of battle, only drums could be heard. Captain Chamberlain echoed the command. As the Continentals moved forward, Asa Abbot turned to his brother and said, "James, we are pushing them back!"

James replied with satisfaction, "That we are Asa, that we are. The Redcoats do know how to retreat."

Washington was observing, with Putnam by his side. "The action is proceeding splendidly, General Putnam. General Greene will soon strike the enemy's right. Perhaps you could provide some encouragement to our right."

Putnam replied, "Indeed, General, I would be most pleased to do so." Putnam cantered off on his horse to the Patriots' right flank.

At the same time, the wounded Hessian was just about to thrust his bayonet into Bellamy's side, but paused when he felt a bayonet point in his ribs. "Hände hoch!" [Hands up] Stroup said firmly. The Hessian was astounded to hear the command in his own language. Stroup was born in America, but his parents had emigrated from Germany. He was fluent in German as well as English. At the same moment, the rest of Bellamy's messmates arrived at the scene.

"Bellamy! Come to your senses man, let him loose!" exclaimed one of the messmates, Corporal Garnett Howard, who realized that Bellamy was out of his head. This was different from a soldier doing his duty. It was murder. Bellamy released the Hessian from his iron grip. The man was unconscious but alive. Howard continued, "Stroup, get the other one behind our lines before Bellamy pins him to a tree." Stroup spoke to the wounded Hessian, "Kommen Sie mit mir ohne Widerstand. Der Mann da drueben will Sie mit dem Bayonett an einen Baum nageln." [You had better come with me peacefully. That man wants to pin you to a tree with your bayonet.] The wounded Hessian's face turned white. All he could do was nod in agreement. Stroup helped the Hessian up and supported him so he could walk with his good leg.

The rest of the troops in the Continental line had now caught up. They stepped over the unconscious Hessian. Howard spoke to another of his messmates Johan Selén, the Swede, "Take Bellamy back to camp. I will keep an eye on this one." Selén slung his musket over his shoulder and walked over to Bellamy, "Justus, you come now. We go back to camp, yah?" Selēn picked up Bellamy's musket and was careful to take him on a different route than Stroup had taken with his prisoner. Bellamy had calmed down. He walked with Selēn in silence, with a glazed look on his face. The unconscious Hessian coughed and came to. His face was a bloody mess. With his musket, Howard motioned for him to get up.

The battle continued to rage on the Patriots' right. The Abbott brothers looked over their shoulders and saw General Putnam giving encouragement, "Keep at it lads, see how the enemy flees before you!" Colonel Hamond had formed his battle line of Redcoats on the edge of the wood that preceded the orchard. He had a clear open area of fire across the buckwheat field. Hessian Grenadiers and more Jaegers had arrived as reinforcements. Captain Wreden and his men had completed the withdrawal out of the wood by the Hollow Way and formed* on the British right along with the other Hessians. No sooner

had Wreden and the troops formed when they were engaged by the Marylanders, the Virginians, the Rangers, and Bellamy's company from the Patriot left.

---

* Formed: A unit moving quickly at the run (March-March), would often lose their tight formation. In the 18th-century military style, men fought shoulder to shoulder in neat ranks. A unit adding itself to a larger formation would have to "form," or align itself on that formation.

CHAPTER FOURTEEN

Irresistible Force

The Continental Army's Advanced Position, the Buckwheat Field, September 16th, 1:40 P.M.

CAPTAIN CHAMBERLAIN WAS handed a note by an aide to General Nixon. Chamberlain read it quickly and addressed the men in his company, "Cease fire! We have just been commanded by General Nixon to flank the enemy. We will lead the assault with Crary's men in support. We are to get as close to the river as possible. Follow me single file! March–March!"

Chamberlain's company headed for the water's edge. Crary's men followed behind. Three more companies took their place on the firing line and kept pressure on the British. The arrival of General Greene's division on the Patriots' left allowed for the shift of the Patriots' right. Finding a clearing in line with the British flank, but out of sight, Chamberlain called a halt, "Form Company! Prime and Load!" The men who had been in single-file formed into two ranks. Crary's men, bringing up the rear, formed also. Quickly and efficiently, they all reloaded. Watching this activity were the British pickets.

Tavington and three other lights were in the wood nearby and opened fire. Two men under Chamberlain's command went down.

Chamberlain gave the command, "Charge bayonets!" The men, who had been at shoulder arms, pivoted their muskets, dropped the muzzle end into their left hands, and gave a resounding cheer, "HUZZA!" Chamberlain continued giving orders, "Run them down boys! March-March!" The men surged forward with their bayonets at the ready. Incredulous, Tavington turned to run. In his haste he got his foot caught between two rocks and his shoe came off, causing him to trip. James Abbot had gotten ahead of the others and saw the Redcoat. He charged toward him. Tavington quickly recovered from his fall and brought his musket around to face the threat. The two men faced off, bayonet to bayonet.

James had only limited training in the use of the bayonet. However, along with his brothers, he had been trained by his father in the military use of the staff, or pole arms. Parrying with his father as a lad, he had often been jabbed in the stomach, until he learned how to block his father's blow. As James closed in on his opponent, Tavington thrust his bayonet toward James's stomach. James blocked the thrust and hit his opponent in the head with his musket butt. Tavington, stunned by the blow, staggered. James swung his musket back and thrust his bayonet into his opponent.

Asa, not as fleet of foot as James, had been running behind James the whole while. He arrived at his brother's side, and said, "James, I saw what happened as I was running. Father's training has proved invaluable."

James removed the bayonet from the limp body, "Yes, Asa, he saved my life."

———◦◉◦———

Behind the British Line in the Buckwheat Field, 2 P.M.

THE LIGHT INFANTRY pickets reported the Rebel flanking maneuver. This was passed onto Colonel Hamond. General Greene's division was putting tremendous pressure on the British right. Captain Prentiss also reported that the Lights and the 42nd Highlanders were out of ammunition. They had been engaged since early that morning. Hamond gave the dreaded command to retreat once again. Loud HUZZAS! were heard up and down the Patriot line. The Crown's forces broke into a run. The Patriots rushed forward to give chase. So, the supposedly invincible British Army could turn and retreat at the run.

Washington, observing the action, saw the danger. The whole British Army was on the other side of the orchard, beyond the wood and buckwheat field. He rode over to General Nixon and exclaimed, "General Nixon, have the men turn about and withdraw to our lines. The action has served its intended purpose. The enemy has been pushed back." Nixon replied, "It shall be done immediately, your Excellency."

It was a new experience and great sport for the Patriots. They had never seen their enemy run from them. Lead elements had just broken out of the orchard near the Jones Farmhouse when they heard the command to withdraw. Reluctantly, they stopped and turned around.

The Jones Farmhouse
(Where the Action Had Started in the Morning)

CAPTAIN MONTRESOR HAD his cannon ready by the Jones Farmhouse. Fresh troops had formed a line of defense. He saw the Lights, the 42nd, and the Hessians climbing over the fence. The Rebels had broken out of the orchard in hot pursuit. Then, to his great surprise, he saw the Rebels turn about and withdraw. Looking over his shoulder, he saw an animated conversation taking place between General Leslie and Colonel Hamond. It did not appear to be going well for Hamond.

The Hollow Way, 2:15 P.M.

WASHINGTON WATCHED THE troops as they made their way back to camp. He noted that they were standing tall, heads held high, with a spring in their step. The battle had obviously sparked their fighting spirit. Lieutenant Colonel Joseph Reed rode up alongside and saluted. Washington returned the salute and commented, "Mr. Reed, it is unfortunate that we did not get to their rear and cut them off as planned. However, the battle ended on a high note. The enemy was pushed backward."

Reed replied, "An officer scouting ahead mistakenly guided us to the flank rather than to the rear. I intervened, but my advice went unheeded."

Washington said, "I have not seen Major Leitch or Lieutenant Colonel Knowlton. How do they fare?"

Reed looked to the ground, "Major Leitch is badly wounded, but it is believed he will recover.* Lieutenant Colonel Knowlton is dead."

Washington replied with shock: "Dead, you say? That is a great loss to our cause. I badly need such gallant men."

---

* Major Andrew Leitch died from his wounds on October 1st. (In sources, see Johnston: P. 78)

CHAPTER FIFTEEN

Campfires

Continental Camp, September 16ᵗʰ, 7 P.M., Sunset

ALL THE CAMPFIRES were burning; the soldiers were finishing the evening meal. It was pork, peas, and biscuits—again. The biscuits were a form of hardtack, baked very hard and dry in order to preserve them. The only way to eat them was to soak them in a stew. The soldiers joked that a biscuit could be run over by a cannon wheel and would not crack. The meal was repetitious, but filling nonetheless. The attitude of the men had changed dramatically from the night before. Where all had been somber yesterday after the terrible defeat, the mood was jovial this night. Laughter could be heard throughout the camp. The victory had transformed morale.

Sergeant Justus Bellamy's messmates were of the same mind. Johan Selēn was telling another one of his stories. The men of the mess—except Bellamy—were laughing. Bellamy usually laughed at Selēn's funny stories, but not tonight. He just kept staring at the fire. Selēn was doing his best to try and snap Bellamy out of his somber mood, but it wasn't working. The officers had taken no disciplinary action against Bellamy for breaking ranks and going after the Hessian alone. What could they say? The officers had abandoned the company the day before on the retreat from the city. It was Bellamy's initiative and leadership that had saved the company from capture.

Garnett Howard spoke to Selēn, "Come on, Johan, let us gather some more firewood at the woodpile." When the two were out of earshot, Howard shared, "I have never seen Justus so upset."

Selēn replied, "He is not himself. I thought I could cheer him up, but no luck."

"I had no idea that the death of Thomas had upset him so much," Howard continued. He was yelling, 'You butchered Thomas' at the Hessian."

Selēn added, "When we retreat on Long Island, Justus had to leave his friend. Something about the battle today must have made him remember."

Howard continued, "Do not give up on your stories. Justus will get over it. He will be his old boisterous self before you know it."

"I pray for him also," Selēn replied.

Howard, somewhat surprised, said, "I did not know you were a praying man."

"I pray when no one is looking," said Selēn, "not to make a show. I have been a Lutheran since boyhood."

"I am a Presbyterian myself," Howard responded. "Well, this explains why I see no fear in you in battle."

Selēn said, "The good Lord is in control."

"Back to the story you were sharing earlier with our messmates," said Howard. "Did your boyhood friends really leave you tied to a tree in a wood back in Sweden?"

"Yah, it was so," said Selēn, "but I will tell you this . . . "

At that same time, General Washington strode with General Nathanael Greene just outside the camp. The men on picket duty were aware of the Generals' presence, but the two men were beyond the sight of the main camp in the growing darkness. Washington was curious about the morale of the men but did not want to create a fuss by walking directly through camp. He wanted the men to relax. Washington addressed Greene, "Mr. Greene, it appears the men are in very good spirits. Quite the change from yesterday, is it not?"

"Yes indeed, your Excellency," Greene replied. "There was no laughter or merriment in the camp yesterday. It was much like a funeral."

Washington went on, "The God of Armies does work in curious ways. All was dismal and defeat yesterday. Only a day later we bask in victory. But now, onto our defensive positions. Even after this reversal, I am sure General Howe will resume his attack in short order."

Greene replied, "With Fort Washington in place to the north, and our entrenchments in depth in front, our position here will be unassailable."

<hr />

Washington's Headquarters, Morris House, 7:30 P.M.

BEFORE RETURNING TO his office to prepare the General Orders for the morning, Washington turned into the stable adjacent to Morris House. Spending time with the horses was always relaxing for him, a way to release the tensions of the day. He found Nelson and Blueskin happily munching their hay. They would yet hear the roaring of many a cannon before the war was over. Washington continued on to his office and sat at his desk. He wrote out the orders for the next day:

GENERAL ORDERS Headquarters, Harlem Heights, September 17th, 1776.

The General most heartily thanks the troops commanded Yesterday, by Major Leitch, who first advanced upon the enemy, and the others who so resolutely supported them— The Behavior of Yesterday was such a Contrast, to that of some Troops the day before, as must show what may be

done, where Officers and Soldiers will exert themselves—
Once more therefore, the General calls upon officers, and
men, to act up to the noble cause in which they are engaged, and to support the Honor and Liberties of their
Country. The gallant and brave Col Knowlton, who would
have been an Honor to any Country, having fallen yesterday, while gloriously fighting, Capt Brown is to take the
Command of the party lately led by Col Knowlton—
Officers and men are to obey him accordingly."

—General Washington

Continental Camp, September 17th, 1776, 5:30 A.M.

JOHN SELĒN WAS chopping kindling with a hatchet. Garnett
Howard was kneeling by the firepit, striking a flint on iron. The
small pile of combustibles caught fire from the spark. Selēn added
kindling to the fire. Stroup had just arrived with a pail of water.
Justus Bellamy added tobacco to his pipe. He lit the pipe with a
small stick from the fire. After taking a puff he addressed the
mess, "At Sergeant's call [a meeting of all sergeants to disseminate
orders to the ranks] later this morning I know what the orders of
the day will be, get ready to dig. Get the entrenching tools ready.
With the thrashing we gave the Redcoats yesterday, I know our
officers will want to dig fortifications to stop a counterattack."

"Selēn, how did you get away?"

Selēn, looking puzzled, replied, "Get away? What do you
mean?"

Bellamy continued, "Back in Sweden, as a young lad. You were
sharing a story last night about how you had been tied to a tree
and left behind in a wood by your friends. Some friends they were.
How did you get free?"

Selēn and Howard looked at each other and smiled knowingly.
Bellamy was back. Selēn went on, "Well, it was like this you see,

we were just young lads playing soldier. I was captured and tied to a tree, all part of the game. They moved on to other things and forgot me. When they got back to the village I was missed. Sven Jorgenson came back and untied me. It was not a moment too soon. It was dark and I heard the wolves howling."

Bellamy answered with disgust, "Lads or not, I cannot believe they left you behind."

Selēn went on to share, "You are right, they were not like the friends I have here. As the scripture says, 'There is a friend that sticks closer than a brother.' I know you fellows would never leave me behind."

Howard shared, "That quote is from Proverbs."

Bellamy solemnly concluded, "No one gets left behind." Then in a more light hearted tone, "Now, let us get on with breakfast, I'm starved. Don't just stand there Stroup, fetch the corn-meal."

———◦◉◦———

"Let all be as a band of Brothers and rise superior to every injury, whether real or imaginary and persevere in the arduous but glorious struggle in which we are engaged, 'till Peace and Independence are secured to our Country."

—George Washington to Anthony Wayne,
September 6th, 1780

CHAPTER SIXTEEN
A Traveler's Contemplation
Mount Vernon, July 4th, 1785, Early Morning

WILLIAM CUNNINGHAM STRODE toward the stable carrying his portmanteau (a cylindrical leather case to carry clothing and other items, to be strapped behind the saddle). He wanted to make an early start toward his next destination. Jasper, the groomsman, came forward with Cunningham's horse under saddle. The blacksmith had just struck the flint against iron to get a spark to start the fire in the forge to begin his work for the day. As Cunningham raised his portmanteau and began strapping it in place behind the saddle, he noticed two figures on horseback. It was the General and Billy Lee.

Washington spoke, "Mr. Cunningham, it is a shame you will not be able to stay for the celebrations."

Cunningham, looking confused, replied, "Celebrations General? I'm afraid I do not follow."

Washington went on, "Why it is July the 4th, Mr. Cunningham. That date in '76 is what we consider the founding of our country. The Declaration of Independence was ratified by Congress."

Cunningham said with a smile, "I dare say King George III is not celebrating this day."

Washington continued, "The Declaration, all very fine words from Mr. Jefferson. From that spark our new nation was forged. However, it is one thing to proclaim independence, it is quite another to earn it. It is the Continental Army which must be remembered, those gallant and persevering men who had resolved to defend the rights of their invaded country so long as the war should continue. It was their sacrifice which kept alive the sacred fire of liberty."

Cunningham mounted his horse and commented, "It was a very costly war for both sides in many ways. Perhaps in peace our countries will find ways to work together."

Washington replied, "Well said, Mr. Cunningham, well said. I hope you find success in your travels."

"Thank you General," Cunningham said, "and once again, your hospitality has been gratefully appreciated. Good day sir."

"Good day," Washington answered.

As Cunningham trotted off, he considered what he had learned of the General and his character from his visit. He thought to himself:

"I was struck with his noble and venerable appearance. It immediately brought to my mind the great part he had acted in the late war. His blue eyes seem to express an air of gravity. Altogether he makes a most noble, respectable appearance, and I really think him the first man in the world [one of the greatest.] After having had management and care of the whole Continental Army, he has now retired without receiving pay for his trouble. He must be a man of great abilities and a strong natural genius, as his master [tutor] never taught him anything but writing and arithmetic.

"It is astonishing the packets of letters that daily come for him from all parts of the world, which employ him most of the morning. The General is remarked for writing a most elegant letter. Like the famous Addison [a playwright], his writing excels his speaking. He never undertakes anything without having first well considered of it and consulted different people, but once he has begun anything, no obstacle or difficulty can come in his way, but what he has determined to surmount.

"Tho' our greatest enemy, I admire him as superior even to the Roman heroes themselves. The General, with a few glasses of champagne, got quite merry, and being with his intimate friends laughed and talked a good deal. Before strangers he is generally reserved, and seldom says a word. I was fortunate in being in his company with his particular acquaintances. I am told during the war he was never seen to smile. The care indeed of such an army was almost enough to make anybody thoughtful and grave. No man but the General could have kept the army together without victuals or clothes; they placed confidence in him that they would have had in no other person. The soldiers, tho' starving at times, in a manner adored him."

General Howe Strikes Back

IN THE AFTERMATH of the battle, General Howe made no move for a month. It appears that the aggressiveness of the Rebels surprised him. He was faced with very strong earthworks to overcome at Har lem Heights and hesitated. But once again, as in the aftermath of the fight in Boston, he struck with a vengeance. Seeing that the fortifications on Harlem Heights were too formidable, he simply bypassed them and landed on the mainland. This threatened to cut off Washington on Manhattan Island. Howe landed on the shoreline of Westchester County on October 12th. The Throgs Neck area was really more of an island than a peninsula, as it was shown on the map used by Howe; it connected to the mainland only at low tide. This misunderstanding of the territory cost Howe several days and gave Washington time to reassess his situation and make good his escape with the army out of Manhattan by the 17th. Washington set a new defensive line at White Plains. He lost to Howe at the battle of White Plains on October 28th.

Fort Washington on Manhattan Island, thought to be impregnable, fell to a combined British and Hessian assault on November 16th.

The Rangers, so critical to the success at the battle of Harlem Heights, were among the 2800 men captured. They suffered terribly on prison ships in the harbor. Many would die in the horrible conditions. Fort Lee across the Hudson was quickly abandoned, with badly needed provisions and equipment left behind. The Hudson was open to British shipping. Only the fortifications and great chain of West Point would prevent their complete control of the whole river during the war.

Washington and the army were chased across New Jersey by Howe. Taking every boat available, and destroying any boat that could not be used, Washington and the army escaped across the Delaware River into Bucks County, Pennsylvania. With the river between him and Howe, Washington had a chance to pause and regroup. His army greatly diminished by desertions, he had few options left. The cause seemed all but lost. But Washington had not forgotten the victory at Harlem Heights. Victory could be pulled out of the jaws of defeat. Against all odds, he launched an amphibious assault across the Delaware to attack an isolated Hessian outpost at Trenton on Christmas Day. This would be the final battle of 1776. But of course that is a story all of its own.

For further information on the crossing of the Delaware and the battle of Trenton see the documentary *America's First D-Day— Washington Crossing* and read the companion book, *Washington's Crossing: America's First D-Day* [Kindle edition], by Robert Child.

To learn more about the project go to the website for the documentary: www.americasfirstdday.com

Justus Bellamy

JUSTUS BELLAMY'S ESCAPE with his men after the fall of New York City and the assistance he provided to General Washington in escaping the British dragoons comes straight out of his pension account. I did add to the account for dramatic effect. As I mentioned in the preface, Bellamy's story could be the basis for a movie in its own right. He was one of the many unsung heroes of the Revolution. I could not fit the account below into the story, but it was so good I had to include here. The editor, who compiled this pension account among others, gave a good background on Bellamy's service. Bellamy's account, following the editor's note, is in his own words.

Editor's Note [Dann]
Justus Bellamy (b. 1757) was born in Cheshire, CT. He answered the alarm after Lexington and Concord, and after one week's service he enlisted on the condition that he and five friends might mess together in Wooster's CT state regiment.

Bellamy was a rough, daring soldier, and General Wooster, while stationed in NY, began to use him for particularly dangerous missions. According to this narrative (his pension application), he and his friends apprehended the Tory (American Loyalist) General Philip Skene at Dobb's Ferry in the summer of 1775.

He took part in the Canadian campaign and served three more terms of service, participating in the battles of Long Island, Harlem Heights, and Danbury, CT. He resided in Vergennes, VT, and Whitehall, NY, after the war. He applied for a pension in 1833. His application was successful.

Bellamy's Account of the Battle of Danbury

Afterwards, and deponent [Bellamy referring to himself] thinks in 1778, when the British were marching on Danbury to destroy it, deponent volunteered with the body of the militia and served under Capt. Ephraim Cook in Col. Thaddeus Cook's regiment. We went to Norwalk in sound. We had a brush with them before they embarked at Compo, were they embarked. At this time one of our adjutants, named Goodrich, got hemmed in by the British on a marsh and was in great danger of being taken, and deponent and thirty men went to his relief. Captain Simon, a British officer, was close in pursuit, but we got Goodrich off clear. In getting off, Captain Simon made a set-to [a brief sharp fight or argument] at this deponent and ordered his men to take deponent. Deponent was left pretty much alone, and deponent drew up his musket and shot Captain Simon down, but afterwards he recovered. Deponent then run and jumped over a fence, and on getting over he found he had fallen in with a large number of British soldiers. He then run to go past a house, when he was fired at in another quarter from a fieldpiece. The ball passed into the house about eight feet above his head, but the hay with which it was wadded hit this deponent on the back of the neck and knocked him over. The first thing the deponent knew after this, he was across the road and over the fence and endeavoring to escape through the orchard. Deponent run three-fourths of a mile under a fence until he come to an inlet from the sound, and when he got there he fell down entirely exhausted.

Still he was shot at but not hurt, and on being rested a little he finished loading his gun and gave his pursuers a shot. Immediately, several guns were fired at deponent, and then deponent escaped and joined his friends. Deponent and friends gave several shots at the British, and then the British all retreated to their ships. Deponent well recollects of hearing that when he was knocked over with the hay wad, that the father of the present United States senator William Foote of Connecticut remarked to the deponent's father that he would never see Justus (this deponent) again. The troops stayed some days watching General Arnold's (the traitor) movements and then returned home."

The character Johan Selen was based on my grandfather.
The artist based the sketch on the photo below.
John M. Selen (1895 – 1971) as a young man.
He was the joy of my early childhood.

List of Characters

All characters—fictional and real—are listed in alphabetical order. "Real" persons, who lived during the time period covered in the book, are indicated with an asterisk.

Abbot, Asa*—Patriot Massachusetts militiaman (brother of James and Phillip).

Abbot, James*—Patriot Massachusetts militiaman (brother of Asa and Phillip).

Abbot, Phillip*—Patriot Massachusetts militiaman, died at the battle of Bunkers Hill (brother of Asa and James).

Aubrey—British regular, lieutenant, light infantryman.

Bacon, Abner*—Patriot Connecticut militia, lieutenant, Knowlton's Rangers.

Baines, Thomas—Patriot Connecticut militia, close friend of Justus Bellamy.

Bangs, Isaac*—Patriot Massachusetts militia, lieutenant.

Bellamy, Justus*—Patriot Connecticut militia, sergeant.

Birch, Samuel*—British regular, lieutenant colonel, commander of the British 17th Light Dragoons.

Blair—British regular, lieutenant, light infantryman.

Braddock—British regular, private, light infantryman.

Brown, Stephen*—Patriot Connecticut militia, captain, Knowlton's Rangers.

Carter*—British regular, Lieutenant (first name unknown.)

Chamberlain, Frank—Patriot Massachusetts militia, captain, the Abbot brothers' company.

Cooke, Henry—Patriot Massachusetts militia, Kempton's Company, Marshall's Regiment.

Crary, Archibald*—Patriot lieutenant colonel, Hitchcock's Rhode Island Regiment.

Cunningham, William—Businessman from Great Britain.

Custis, George Washington Parke*—Stepgrandson of George Washington.

Darby—British regular, private in British 17th Light Dragoons.

Derry—British regular, private in British 17th Light Dragoons.

Gates, Horatio*—Patriot general.

Grant, James*—British regular, general.

Greene, Nathanael*—Patriot general.

Gridley—British regular, private in British 17th Light Dragoons.

Griffin—British regular, private in British 17th Light Dragoons.

Hamond, Ashley—British regular, colonel, light infantryman.

Hobbs, Lionel—British regular, sergeant, light infantryman.

Howard, Garnett—Patriot Connecticut militia, corporal, Bellamy's company.

Howe, William*—British regular, general, overall commander of British forces in Boston.

Jasper—Groomsman at Mount Vernon.

Jones—British regular, sergeant in British 17th Light Dragoons.

Knowlton, Thomas*—Patriot Connecticut militia, lieutenant colonel, Knowlton's Rangers.

Knox, Henry*—Patriot colonel, commander of all Continental artillery.

Lee, Billy (Will) *—Slave, personal servant of George Washington.

Leitch, Andrew*—Patriot major, Weedon's 3rd Virginia Regiment.

Leslie, Alexander*—British regular, general, commander of the light troops.

Lilie, Stuart—British regular, private in British 17th Light Dragoons.

Loftus, William*—British regular, lieutenant in British 17th Light Dragoons.

Monroe, James*—Patriot lieutenant, 3rd Virginia Regiment, 5th President of the United States.

Montresor, John*—British regular, captain, senior military engineer.

Nash—British regular, private in British 17th Light Dragoons.

Nixon John*—Patriot general.

Page, Thomas*—British regular, lieutenant, one of General Howes's aides-de-camp.

Prentiss, Arthur—British regular, captain, light infantryman.

Putnam, Israel*—Patriot general.

Reed, Joseph*—Patriot, lieutenant colonel, one of General Washington's aides-de-camp.

Robertson, Archibald*—British regular, captain, military engineer.

Rose, William—Patriot artilleryman, lieutenant, commander of a gun crew.

Selēn, Johan—Patriot Connecticut militia, private, Bellamy's company.

Shulham, Molyneux*—Vice-Admiral of the Blue and Commander in Chief of His Britannic Majesty's Ship in North America.

Smith—British regular, private in British 17th Light Dragoons.

Smith, Francis*—British regular, general.

Soper, Amasa*—Patriot Massachusetts militia, sergeant, Kempton's Company, Marshalls Regiment.

Stroup—Patriot Connecticut militia, private, Bellamy's company.

Stuart, Charles*—British regular, captain, military engineer.

Tavington, Percival—British regular, private, light infantry.

Thomas, John*—Patriot general.

Thomas, John*—Son of the general.

Thorp, David*—Patriot Connecticut militia, sergeant, Knowlton's Rangers.

Tilghman, Tench*—Patriot, lieutenant colonel, one of General Washington's aides-de-camp.

Trumbull, John*—Patriot major, one of General Washington's aides-de-camp.

Washington, George*—Patriot general, commander-in-chief of the Continental Army.

Washington, William*—Patriot captain, Weedon's 3rd Virginia Regiment. A kinsman of George Washington.

Wilson—British regular, corporal in British 17th Light Dragoons.

Winchester—British regular, private in British 17th Light Dragoons.

Von Wreden*—Hessian Jaeger captain (full name unknown.)

End Notes

Notations without quotations and with no sources listed are commentaries from the author. For the notations that include quotations that were drawn directly from historical sources, the quotations appear here exactly as they do in the original sources. In the narrative, these quotations may have been changed slightly to suit the flow of the story. This accounts for some minor discrepancies between the content of the narrative and the content of the end notes. Complete information on cited references is provided in the sources section that follows.

—Chapter One—

Page 7
"Nelson, now 22 years of age...Have heard the roaring of many a cannon in their time...Blueskin was not the favorite, on account of his not standing fire so well as the venerable old Nelson. The General makes no manner of use of them now; he keeps them here in a nice stable, where they feed away at their ease for their

past services" (Hunter, p. 80). The character William Cunningham is based on Robert Hunter, Jr. In his diary, Hunter made interesting and insightful comments on Mount Vernon and the character of George Washington.

"The General accepted the surrender...on Nelson" (Custis).

> The horses which he rode, in the war of Independence, were said to be superb. We have a perfect remembrance of the charger which bore him in the greatest of his triumphs, when he received the sword of the vanquished, on the ever memorable 19th October, 1781. It was a chestnut, with white face and legs, and was called Nelson, after the patriotic Governor of Virginia. Far different was the fate of this favorite horse of Washington, from that of "the high mettled racer." When the Chief had relinquished its back, it was never mounted more, but cropped the herbage in summer, was housed and well cared for in winter, often caressed by the master's hand, and died of old age at Mount Vernon, many years after the Revolution. (Custis)

"Washington's affection for the horse was reciprocated. It is said that, as George Washington would walk around the grounds of the estate, **he would stop at Nelson's paddock, 'when the old warhorse would run, neighing, to the fence, proud to be caressed by the great master's hands'.**" (Thompson, p. 59).

Page 8
"[My father is a] Scottish merchant living in London. [I have been tasked with collecting overdue debts...travels have taken me from] Canada to New York, Pennsylvania, Maryland, and Virginia. [I am bound for] North and South Carolina" (Wright and Tinling).

"A defaulter is worse than a common pickpocket" (Washington Papers, George Washington to Thomas Jefferson, July 6, 1796). In

Washington's exact words, "Nero; a notorious defaulter; or even to a common pick-pocket."

Page 9
"In conversation he looks you full in the face" (Flexner, p. 192). Flexner cites "Observations of Washington as a young man by George Mercer, a fellow officer in the VA Regiment in 1758."

> In conversation he looks you full in the face, is deliberate, deferential, and engaging. His demeanor at all times composed and dignified. His movements and gestures are graceful, his walk majestic, and he is a splendid horseman. (Flexner, p. 192)

"I rode by the General's side throughout the entire war (Mount Vernon website)**, and we seldom speak of it."** One of the historians who read my manuscript challenged this point, asking, "Was it true that Washington seldom spoke of the war?" My purpose in including this exchange was to highlight that fact that many veterans seldom speak of their wartime experiences and to show that Billy Lee rode by Washington's side throughout the war. I also wanted to demonstrate Billy Lee's intimate knowledge of Washington.

In his book *Washington: A Life,* Ron Chernow describes the countless visitors who stopped in at Mount Vernon after the war, hoping to hear the General tell battlefield stories: "[Washington's] modesty disappointed those who expected him to narrate the wartime drama especially for them" (Chernow, p. 469).

It is common knowledge that veterans seldom speak of their wartime experiences. My father, John Koopman, Jr., served with the U.S. Army in the South Pacific during World War II. He rarely spoke of it, and when he did he offered a sanitized version in which he left out the violence. I had the honor of getting to know a coworker who was in the U.S. Marines at the siege of Khe Sanh. It was one of the most intense battles of the Vietnam War. He would tell me about it, but like my father, he offered a sanitized version. This reluctance is clearly depicted in the online article, "Why Are Veterans Reluctant to Discuss Their War Experiences?" (http://www.wisegeek.com/why-are-veterans-reluctant-to-discuss-their-war-experiences.htm#didyouknowout.)

Here are some excerpts:

> [T]hose veterans who served in a war are sometimes reluctant to discuss their experiences, and there can be a number of reasons why this is the case [such as] not wanting to upset loved ones, especially wives or children.

> About 88% of veterans returning from a war have had direct experience of violence: witnessing it, being victim to it, or causing it. Many have been in daily fear of their lives for a period of time. The environment of distrusting all but fellow soldiers is a difficult one to shake when coming home, and a number of vets experience some degree of posttraumatic stress syndrome.

> [T]here may be great reluctance to discuss what occurred because veterans are trying to let go of that environment and reintegrate into a world where there is more ability to trust and greater safety. Reliving the experiences may make this difficult, or so many soldiers may feel.

Now, what about Washington? As commander-in-chief, he led from the front during battle—not from a remote headquarters. As a young man in the French and Indian War, he witnessed particularly brutal, personal combat. This is alluded to in Chapter 3, "The Unveiling." A British column was cut to pieces in an ambush by the French and their Native American allies. George Washington was the last officer still standing and led a fighting retreat, saving many lives. Here is a quote in his own words describing what he experienced:

> The shocking scenes which presented themselves in this Night's March are not to be described. The dead, the dying, the groans, lamentation, and cries along the Road of the wounded for help were enough to pierce a heart of adamant [meaning unyielding, hard]. (Anderson, p. 20)

There were exceptions, but in general, Washington was reluctant to open up to a stranger about anything. As Robert Hunter, an astute eye witness, observed, "Before strangers he is generally reserved, and seldom says a word" (Hunter, p. 79). Chernow stated, "While Washington opened up in Hunter's company, he clammed up with others" (Chernow, p. 468).

A fascinating observation was made by the General's stepgrandson, George Washington Parke Custis, about Washington's behavior after his retirement from the presidency: "He would frequently, when sitting with his family, appear absent; his lips would move, his hand [would] be raised, and he would evidently seem under the influence of thoughts, which had nothing to do with the quiescent scene around him" (Custis).

Where was Washington's mind at such moments? Custis does not speculate. Was Washington reliving a battle? It seems likely, but we can't know for sure.

For those who have an opportunity to listen to a veteran describe wartime experiences and would like advice on how to listen and respond, I recommend Al Siebert's "Guidelines for Listening to War Veterans" (http://www.resiliencycenter.com/articles/Vetlist.shtml).

Here is a summary of the points Siebert makes:

1. Don't ask about a person's experiences unless you can handle honest answers.
2. Give the person lots of time.
3. Be an active listener. Ask for details. Ask about feelings.
4. Remain quiet if he or she starts crying.

5.   Listen with empathy, but minimize sympathy.

6.   Ask if he or she sees anything positive about being in combat. The same extreme circumstances that cause emotional trauma for some people cause others to become stronger.

"Washington gave him (Cunningham) a personal tour…wartime letters" (Wright and Tinling).

Page 10
"[N]oticed his grandfather leaving the house at an unusually late hour and wanted to know where he was going. This was not his grandfather's routine" (Custis).

> About sunrise, General Washington invariably visited and inspected his stables. He was very fond of horses, and his equipages were always of a superior order. (Custis)

—Chapter Two—

Page 11
"Abigail Adams reported being able to hear the cannon fire from 10 miles away" (McCullough, p. 91).

Rammer, matross, fixed shot, piece, and lint stock.

The rammer, a wooden pole, had two different functions. One end had a plug close in diameter to the bore of the barrel, to push the cartridge to the end, or breech, of the cannon. The other end, called the sponge, was wrapped in lambskin, with the wool facing out. After 12 or so firings of the cannon, the sponge would be dipped in a bucket of water. The sponge would then be run down the barrel several times to cool it off (Greene, pp. 370 and 375).

"The matross's duty who: carries the haversack, mans the drag ropes, carries the side boxes of the pieces" (Stevens, p. 45).

"The matross who carries the haversack (shoulder bag), ought to be a pretty stout and strong man, as the fatigue of carrying the ammunition to serve the piece in the field is considerable" (Stevens, pp. 56–57).

Matross: A soldier who assists artillery gunners in loading, firing, sponging, and moving the guns (Boatner, p. 686).

"Fixed shot is a bag of gunpowder attached to a cannon ball. The assembly is then referred to as "the cartridge" . . . fixed ammunition that combined ball and propellant into one unit" (Greene, p. 371).

"Piece" is synonymous with "cannon."

A lint stock is a wooden pole with a slow burning fuse (slow match) attached on the end, essentially a large candle wick. The slow match is, "[A] 3 strand cotton rope impregnated with saltpeter and treated with lead acetate and lye to burn at a rate of 5 inches an hour" (Greene, p. 375).

I would like to give special thanks to Jim Stinson, president of Proctor's Artillery Company, and John Mills, captain of Mott's Artillery and curator of the Princeton Battlefield. Both provided invaluable input on the artillery segment.

Cannon fire commands (Stevens, pp. 63–64).

Cannon came in different sizes based on the weight of the cannonball used. A 6-pound cannon (known as a 6 pounder) fired a 6-pound cannonball. Cannon could also fire "canister"—a container full of large musket balls. The canister would act much like a shotgun and was used against troops at close range—within 100 yards. The range for a cannon ball would be approximately 1.5 miles. The type of cannon bombarding Boston would have been intended for use in the field, mounted on wagon wheels.

Cannon operated on much the same principle as muskets. The canon was a long tube that had a closed end, or breech. Projectiles had to be rammed down the tube with a rammer. The gunpowder would be first, followed by the projectile. A small vent hole would be located near the breech 90 degrees offset (perpendicular) to the tube. Additional gunpowder poured into the vent hole would contact the powder loaded inside. Igniting the powder in the vent hole would in turn ignite the powder in the breech. The explosion would then push the projectile out of the tube at high velocity.

At full strength, each cannon would have a total of 13 men in support of it. Under the British system emulated by the Americans: "The service of a field piece, whose caliber is an eight pounder, managed by eight men of the royal artillery, and five men of the infantry." (Stevens, p. 57)

"Protected by a leather thumb-piece"

> The thumb-piece . . . was very important to prevent burns to the gunner (bombardier) who stopped up the vent during the loading procedure . . . the thumb-piece was a kind of small bag, about 3 inches square, made of strong skin or leather, and stuffed with hair: one of the sides is recovered with a piece of leather, so that the cannoneer may lodge his fingers in it while stopping the vent. (Greene, p. 374)

Page 12
Major John Trumbull, one of the sons of Governor Jonathan Trumbull of Connecticut. Later in life, John Trumbull would receive the title, "Painter of the American Revolution." The original paintings in his Revolutionary War series hang in the U.S. Capitol Rotunda.

Page 13
"[D]ivert the enemy's attention from our real design" (Harris, p. 62).

Page 14

"The Great Bridge" (Beck). Also known as "Cambridge Bridge." See a map and the routes of Dawes' and Revere's respective Rides at http://allthingsliberty.com/2014/04/dissecting-the-timeline-of-paul-reveres-ride/. Here is an excerpt from Beck's commentary:

> Dr. Warren did not have the definite evidence of a British march, and was loath to send another alarm since he had already sent Revere out on two false alarms in the previous days. Hence, Dawes rode off with no particular urgency, taking the circuitous road from Boston Neck gate and through Roxbury, west through Brighton, up the Great Bridge across the Charles River (where the Anderson Memorial Bridge is now), through Cambridge center, then up what is essentially Massachusetts Avenue, all the way to the Rev. Jonas Clarke home in Lexington, where Samuel Adams and John Hancock were hiding out. Comparing old maps and overlaying them to modern mapping tools, this total distance was about 16.5 miles, and there is no evidence that Dawes alerted anyone along the way. After all, he had left when nothing was confirmed.

"Head out down that road and find John Goddard, the wagon master..." Much of the raw materials for the prefabricated fortifications for Dorchester Heights came from John Goddard's farm in Brookline (Harris, p. 68). He was a Son of Liberty.

"Each was slightly shorter than average height but powerfully built."

> Will, the huntsman, better known in Revolutionary lore as Billy, rode a horse called Chinkling, a surprising leaper, and made very much like its rider, low, but sturdy, and of great bone and muscle. Will had but one order, which was to keep with the hounds; and, mounted on Chinkling . . .

this fearless horseman would rush, at full speed, through brake or tangled wood, in a style at which modern huntsmen would stand aghast. (Thompson, p. 54)

Page 15
"2,000 [select] men" (McCullough, p. 92).

"Eight hundred men, mostly riflemen, took up positions along the shore" (McCullough, p. 92).

"[T]hen the carts with the entrenching tools; after that the main working body under General Thomas consisting of 1200; a train of more than 300 carts loaded with facines, pressed hay, in bundles of seven or eight hundred, closed the procession" (Gordon letter, p. 362).

Page 16
"[T]hose barrels are filled with rocks and sand" (Harris, p. 62).

Page 17
"The Heights are steep and free of any trees or brush" (Harris, p. 62).

"[O]nly enough gunpowder to supply 9 cartridges per soldier, only 36 barrels" (Harris, p. 15).

"Mr. Elbridge Gerry" (Boatner, pp. 430–31). Gerry, who was from Marblehead, Massachusetts, was one of the signers of the Declaration of Independence.

"I made it known that there were really 1800 barrels of powder" (Bell).

Bible verses
Four people read the rough draft of the manuscript for the book.

Two of the four had the same question: Did Washington quote the Bible? A fair question. The answer is most certainly yes.

Although I cannot find a reference to these particular scriptures in the Washington Papers, Washington did quote from the Bible in his writings on many occasions. My purpose in this part of the story was threefold. First, I wanted to communicate the loneliness of command for Washington. For national security purposes, he had to keep much to himself. Second, I wanted to show how a person of faith could justify lying without compromising their beliefs. Hence, lie to save lives. The incident with Rahab demonstrates that principle. Third, I wanted to point out that Washington was in fact well-versed in scripture. Dr. Peter Lillback has listed several hundred paraphrases, allusions to, and direct quotes by George Washington from the Bible in his book *George Washington's Sacred Fire*, Appendix II, beginning on page 739). For a more in-depth discussion on this topic, please visit my website at www.johnkoopmaniii.com. Click "Articles," then select "George Washington and the Bible."

Page 18
"Many of the carts made three trips, some four; for a vast quantity of materials had been collected, especially chandeliers and facines" (Harris, p. 65).

"[Three hundred and sixty] 360 ox teams" (Harris, p. 64).

"Hundreds of soldiers . . . Lieutenant Colonel Rufus Putnam . . . chandeliers in a military engineering book, *Muller's Field Engineer*" (paraphrased from McCullough, p. 88).

"John my boy, how in the world did you get past the sentries?" (Thomas letter). Actual quote from a letter General Thomas wrote to his wife: "Your son John is well and in high spirits. He ran away from Oakley [family servant] privately, on Tuesday morning, and got by the sentries and came to me on Dorchester Hills, where he has been most of the time since."

Page 19
"At 3 A.M. the initial assault force was relieved by replacements"
(McCullough, p. 93).

—Chapter Three—

Page 21
". . . began their bombardment at 11 in the evening on the first
two nights and yet began at 7 in the evening last night" (Harris,
pp. 62–63).

Page 22
"I have purposely left it open to the Rebels."

> ...there was no danger from it [the Rebels occupying the
> Heights], and that it was to be wished that the rebels
> would take possession of it, as they could be dislodged.
> (McCullough, pp. 70–71)

Page 23
"I fought with him on the ill-fated Braddock expedition."
Montresor was only one of many men of note at the Battle of
Monongahela in addition to George Washington who would play
a role in the American War of Independence (AWI) years later. Also
present were Daniel Boone (frontiersman), Daniel Morgan (AWI
Patriot general), Horatio Gates (AWI Patriot general), and Thomas
Gage (AWI military Royal governor of Massachusetts 1774 -
1775).

Page 24
"Two horses were shot from under him and yet he remained un-
scathed" (George Washington to his mother, Mary Ball Washington,
July 18, 1755, Washington Papers).

> I luckily escaped without a wound, though I had four bul-
> lets through my coat, and two horses shot under me.
> (Washington Papers)

Washington not only had two horses shot out from under him and four bullet holes in his coat, but two bullets also passed through his hat:

> The hat worn on that eventful day, and which was pierced
> by two balls, was at Mount Vernon. (Custis)

"Appeared more like magic than the work of human beings" (Harris, p. 65).

Page 25
"The rebels have done more in one night than my whole army would have done in months" (Gordon letter, p. 363).

Lieutenant Carter commented, "The Rebels now command old Boston entirely: the enemy must inevitably be driven from thence, or we must abandon the town" (Harris, p. 65). Unfortunately, the account does not mention Carter's first name.

Abbot brothers. In my research I had come across the mention of the death of Phillip Abbot at the battle of Bunker's Hill (see note below). Further investigation brought me to the Abbot family website. Although their motivation for enlisting is unknown, I thought it would be compelling to have the brothers join up to avenge Phillip's death. I cannot place them at the siege of Boston, but they did serve in the New York campaign. The timeline makes it possible for them to have served at both Boston and New York. It is unknown whether they out stayed their original period of enlistment.

The information below on Asa and James is from the Abbot family genealogy, available at http://abbottfamily.weebly.com/revolutionary-war-1775-1783.html.

"**Asa Abbott,** born 1756, fought in the Revolutionary War with Captain Jeremiah Mason's Company, Connecticut . . . enlisted January 26, 1776, for two months to go to Brooklyn, New York."

James Abbot, corporal, "enlisted January 26, 1776, with Captain Jeremiah Mason's Company, Connecticut, for two months to go to Brooklyn."

Phillip Abbot was killed at the Battle of Bunker's Hill on June 17, 1775. A list of those killed in battle is available at the Sons of the American Revolution website, http://www.revolutionarywararchives. org/bunkerfallen.html.

Page 26
"The General said to remember it is the fifth of March, and avenge the death of your brethren" (Gordon letter, p. 363).

"[U]tmost consternation" (George Washington to Charles Lee, March 14, 1776. Washington Papers). This was the reaction in Boston to seeing the surprise fortifications on Dorchester Heights.

"Major General Israel Putnam was to lead an amphibious assault" (Address to the Continental Congress, March 7, 1776, Washington Papers). The following is an excerpt from Washington's address to Congress:

> Four thousand chosen men who were held in readiness, were to ... have embarked at the mouth of Cambridge River in two divisions; The first under the command of Brig. Genl. Sullivan, the second under Brig. Genl. Greene, the whole to have been commanded by Major General Putnam. The first

division was to land at the Powder House and gain possession of Bacon Hill and Mount Horam. The second at Barton's Point or a little South of it, and after securing that post, to join the other division and force the Enemy's Works and Gates for letting in the Roxbury Troops.

"60 boats" (McCullough, p. 89).

"50 men each" (McCullough, p. 53).

Page 27
"The gates would then be opened to allow more troops in from Roxbury" (Harris, p. 66).

—Chapter Four—

Page 29
"Rebels have improvised a reversal, which he finds alarming and unexpected. His ships cannot possibly remain in the harbor under the fire of the batteries from Dorchester Heights" (Harris, p. 65). Dorchester Neck includes the Heights.

Page 30
"A most astonishing night's work . . . must have employed from 15,000 to 20,000 men" (Captain Archibald Robertson's diary, in Harris, p. 65).

"In a situation so critical, I have determined upon an immediate attack with all the force I can transport" (letter from Howe to Lord Dartmouth, in Harris, p. 65).

"Five regiments are to embark immediately on five transports at Long Wharf. . . . The attack is to be made with the bayonet" (paraphrased from Harris, pp. 65–66).

General Howe's orderly book with details of the attack fell into Patriot hands when the British departed Boston. Rev. Gordon was able to view the contents (Gordon letter, p. 364).

> The storm hindered the attack; and it was so given out afterward, in general orders by Gen. How[e] as appears by one of the orderly books that fell into our hands. (Gordon letter, p. 364)

"Long Wharf." A still-extant though much-shortened pier on Boston Harbor.

"Castle William." Today known as Castle Island. During the Revolutionary War, it was a small island to the east of Dorchester Heights. Today it is attached to the mainland. A significant stone fort, built in the 1800s, still stands there. Its predecessor, Castle William, was a much more modest fort. The British kept a small garrison there throughout the siege.

"Four elite battalions, two of grenadier and two of light infantry." A typical British regiment at the time numbered between 400 and 500 men made up of 10 companies. Most were called "Hat Companies." They wore the typical cocked hat of the day and were regular infantry. A regiment would also have a grenadier company and a light infantry (LI) company.

The grenadiers had stopped using grenades, as they did in the French and Indian war, but they retained the title. They were made up of seasoned veterans who were the tallest among their peers. They wore bearskin hats that came to a point, as seen in many paintings. Tall men already, the intentionally added height of the hat made them seem even taller and more intimidating. The LI company was made up of young and athletic men. They were meant to be quick and nimble in battle. The LI wore leather helmets. They were often issued leather breaches rather than cloth for protection from brush, since they were frequently tasked with going through

rough terrain. Many times the grenadier and LI companies were taken from their regiments to form elite battalions that were used as shock troops at a critical point in battle.

". . . a feint toward Lechmere Point" (Gordon letter, p. 364).

"General Pigott to remain in Boston with 600 men . . . to guard against attack" (Gordon letter, p. 365).

Page 31
". . . all the ladders that can be procured are to be cut into ten foot lengths" (Gordon letter, p. 365).

"Grant, a member of the House of Commons, had boasted that with 5,000 British regulars he could march from one end of the American continent to the other." (McCullough, p. 6)

"There was never a doubt of General Howe's desire to attack. . . We shall soon push the rebels off the heights" (McCullough, p. 97).

Page 32
"I have already spoken with two lieutenant colonels, two majors, and three captains" (Captain Archibald Robertson's diary, in Harris, p. 67).

"This assault is nothing less than suicidal madness" (paraphrased from McCullough, p. 94).

"I think the most serious step ever an army of this strength in such a situation took considering the state of the Rebels' works...and the number of men they appear to have under arms. The fate of this whole army and the town is at stake not to say the fate of America" and "ought to immediately embark" (Harris, p. 67).

Page 33
"They looked in general pale and dejected, and said to one another

that it would be another Bunker's Hill affair or worse" (Gordon letter, p. 364).

"We saw distinctly the preparations which the enemy was making to dislodge us. The entire waterfront of Boston lay open to our observation, and we saw the embarkation of troops from the various wharfs. We were in high spirits, well prepared to receive the threatened attack" (McCullough, p. 95).

"We had at least 20 pieces of artillery mounted on [the Heights], amply supplied with ammunition. We waited with impatience for the attack, when we meant to emulate, and hoped to eclipse, the glories of Bunker's Hill" (Harris, p. 67).

Page 34
"As the Season is now fast approaching, when every man must expect to be drawn into the Field of action, it is highly necessary that he should prepare his mind, as well as everything necessary for it. It is a noble Cause we are engaged in, it is the Cause of virtue, and mankind, every temporal advantage and comfort to us, and our posterity, depends upon the Vigor of our exertions; in short, Freedom, or Slavery must be the result of our conduct, there can therefore be no greater Inducement to men to behave well…. Next to the favor of divine providence, nothing is more essentially necessary to give this Army the victory over all its enemies, than Exactness of discipline, Alertness when on duty, and Cleanliness in their arms and persons…" (George Washington, February 27, 1776, General Orders, in Washington Papers).

Page 35
"…our officers and men appeared impatient for the appeal, and to have possessed the most animated sentiments and determined spirit" (George Washington to the Continental Congress, Cambridge, March 7, 1776, in Washington Papers).

". . . three floating batteries [will proceed] in front of the other boats and keep up a heavy fire on that part of the town where our men are to land....The plan [is] well digested, and as far as I can judge from the cheerfulness and alacrity which distinguishes the officers and men who are to engage in the enterprise, I [have] reason to hope for a favorable and happy issue" (George Washington to the Continental Congress, March 7, 1776, in Washington Papers).

Page 36
"The tide had ebbed. The winds from the gathering storm blew harder. The direction had changed; it was now blowing west directly against the British transports traveling from Boston to Castle William" (Harris, p. 66–67).

—Chapter Five—

Page 37
"The storm had increased in power. The winds were hurricane force and accompanied by snow and sleet" (McCullough, p. 96).

"...advised [against] the going off altogether. Lord Percy and some others seconded him [General Howe] and that the general said it was his own sentiments from the first, but thought the honor of the troops concerned" (Captain Archibald Robertson's Diary, in Harris, p. 67).

"...the weather continuing to be boisterous the next day and night gave the enemy time to improve their works...wherefore [Howe] judged it most advisable to prepare for the evacuation of the town" (letter from General Howe to Lord Dartmouth, in Harris, p. 68).

Page 38
"Why they had not done it that day, if they ever intended it, God only knows. For my part, I should have been willing to have received

them either by night or day, as we had a tolerable cover from musketry, and as to their field pieces they could not have brought them to bear because of the situation of the ground. Had they been so rash they would in all probability have found the 5th of March, 1776, more bloody on their side than Preston made the same day in 1770 on ours. In fine, I can't think it was ever their design more than to make a parade. But they had good excuse, [last night was] the most violent storm of wind & rain mixed with snow & hail that ever I was exposed to" (Isaac Bangs in his own words, in Bangs letter).

Page 39
"[A] day of fasting and prayer": (George Washington, General Orders Head Quarters, Cambridge, March 6, 1776, in Washington Papers). Here is the full unedited quote, followed by an explanation:

> Thursday the seventh Instant, being set apart by the Honourable the Legislature of this province, as a day of fasting, prayer, and humiliation, "to implore the Lord, and Giver of all victory, to pardon our manifold sins and wickedness's, and that it would please him to bless the Continental Arms, with his divine favour and protection"—All Officers, and Soldiers, are strictly enjoined to pay all due reverence, and attention on that day, to the sacred duties due to the Lord of hosts, for his mercies already received, and for those blessings, which our Holiness and Uprightness of life can alone encourage us to hope through his mercy to obtain.

Washington was, in essence, ordering the army to fast and pray. The quote within Washington's orders ("to implore . . . protection") was from the resolution of the Massachusetts legislature. It was common among legislatures at the time to proclaim a day of fasting and prayer during times of difficulty and celebration. The concept of fasting and prayer is rooted in the Bible. Citizens were encouraged to attend church and to fast for the entire day to remain focused on prayer.

Another instance of the practice of prayer and fasting comes from a diary entry by Washington in 1774: "June 1ˢᵗ. Went to Church & fasted all day."

Editors Jackson and Twohig (see Sources) note the following on Washington's diary entry on that day of June 1774:

> This service was pursuant to the resolution passed on 24 May for a day of fasting, humiliation, and prayer to symbolize Virginia's solidarity with the people of Boston, and many of the Virginia parishes joined in the observance. In this service at Bruton Parish Church, Rev. Thomas Price, chaplain of the House of Burgesses, preached on the destruction of the city of Sodom, taking for his text the answer to Abraham's question to the Lord: "Wilt thou also destroy the righteous with the wicked?" And he answered, "I will not destroy it for ten's sake. (Gen. 18:23, 32)

Page 10
"It came through our lines at Boston Neck by flag of truce…no official recognition should be afforded the appeal" (paraphrased from Harris, p. 68).

"As it was Colonel Ebenezer Learned who received the letter from the Ministerialists, I shall have him establish contact with them in the morning. He will explain that the letter was received by me, and that as it is an unauthenticated letter, I will take no notice of it. Any understanding between our camps will be strictly tacit" (paraphrased from Harris, p. 68).

"Regardless of the report . . . 3 barrels of powder" (George Washington to Continental Congress, March 7, 1776, in Washington Papers). Here is the unedited version of Washington's statement:

Notwithstanding the report from Boston that Halifax is the place of their Destination, I have no doubt but that they are going to the Southward of this, and I apprehend to New York. Many reasons lead me to this Opinion, It is in some measure corroborated by their sending an express Ship there which on Wednesday Week got on shore and bilged at Cape Cod. The Dispatches if written were destroyed when she was boarded; she had a parcel of Coal and about 4000 Cannon Shot, six Carriage Guns, 1 or 2 Swivels and three Barrels of Powder.

"**Carriage guns.**" As explained by Muller (pp. 95 and 99), cannon were mounted on two types of structures. Cannon for use on ships were mounted on a structure with four very small wheels, easily moved on deck but not on rough terrain. This type would also be used inside forts and were called "Garrison Carriages." For use on roads and fields were "Travelling Carriages." Cannon were mounted on a structure with two wagon size wheels. Washington does not specify the type of gun carriage. They were most likely travelling carriages. This must have been why he surmised that this was part of the buildup for the attack on New York City. To move inland after a landing, the British troops would require artillery support beyond their navy. The other items: "Shot" being cannon balls, and "Powder" being gunpowder to fire the shot out of the cannon.

"**On March the 1ˢᵗ, Congress directed General Lee to take over the Southern Department at Charleston, South Carolina**" (Hickman).

"**Before his arrival with 3,000 men…perhaps out of concern to damaging the property of Loyalists in the city**" (paraphrased from Shuldham, pp. 109–112).

"**I shall hold the Riflemen and other parts of our Troops in readiness to march at a Moment's warning and Govern my movements by the** events that happen, or such Orders as I may receive from Congress, which I beg may be ample and forwarded with all possible expedition"(George Washington to Continental Congress, March 7, 1776, in Washington Papers).

—Chapter Six—

Page 44
"Greene is as dangerous as Washington. I never feel secure when encamped in his neighborhood" (Hayball).

—Chapter Seven—

Page 47
"He held his head in his hands, pondering the horrors of the day." Washington's actual situation report in the aftermath of the Continental Army's inglorious retreat:

> But in the Morning they began their operations. Three Ships of War came up the North River, as high as Bloomingdale, which put a total Stop to the removal by Water of any more of our Provision &ca. and about Eleven O'Clock those in the East River began a most severe and heavy Cannonade to scour the Grounds and cover the landing of their Troops between Turtle Bay and the City, where Breast Works had been thrown up to oppose them; as soon as I heard the firing, I road with all possible dispatch towards the place of landing, when to my great surprize and mortification, I found the Troops that had been posted in the Lines, retreating with the utmost precipitation, and those ordered to support them, Parsons's and Fellows's Brigades, flying in every direction and in the greatest confusion, notwithstanding the exertions of their Generals to form them. I used every means in my power, to rally and get them into some order, but my attempts were fruitless and ineffectual and on the appearance of a small

party of the Enemy, not more than Sixty or Seventy in Number, their disorder increased and they ran away in the greatest confusion without firing a single Shot. Finding that no confidence was to be placed in these Brigades and apprehending that another part of the Enemy might pass over to Harlem plains and cut of the retreat to this place, I sent orders to secure the Heights in the best manner with the Troops that were stationed on and near them, which being done; the retreat was effected with but little or no loss of Men, tho' of a considerable part of our Baggage occasioned by this disgraceful and dastardly conduct We are now Encamped with the Main body of the Army on the Heights of Harlem, where I should hope the Enemy would meet with a defeat in case of an Attack, If the generality of our Troops would behave with tolerable resolution, But, experience, to my extreme affliction, has convinced me that this is rather to be wished for than expected. However I trust that there are many who will act like men and shew themselves worthy of the blessings of Freedom. I have sent out some reconoitring parties to gain Intelligence if possible, of the disposition of the Enemy and shall inform Congress of every material event by the earliest Opportunity. (George Washington to the President of Congress, September 16, 1776, in Washington Papers)

"Are these the men with which I am to defend America?" (McCullough, p. 212).

"Washington had nearly been captured in the morning near Kip's Bay, early in the invasion. He could not stop the Connecticut Militia from running away from the enemy. He sat on his horse, frozen in discouragement, until his staff came on the scene and led his horse away by the reins" (McCullough, p. 213).

Page 48

"Birch was in command of the 17th during the New York campaign." The regiment's motto was "Death or Glory" (http://www. 17ld.blogspot.com/p/history.html).

Page 49

Horses and lead changes.

Thoroughbred horses are bred specifically for racing. They are also good jumpers. The Thoroughbred was not common in America during the Revolution. It is not known what type of horse Nelson was. Horses such as Nelson that were used for foxhunting were simply called Hunters. The Quarter Horse breed was also in America at the time. The name comes from their speed in racing in the quarter mile. A powerful sprinter, a Quarter Horse will beat a Thoroughbred in a quarter-mile race. The Thoroughbred, bred for racing the mile, overtakes the Quarter Horse after the quarter-mile. The 17th Light Dragoons did bring Thoroughbreds from England. For the purposes of the story, Nelson was given the characteristics of a Quarter Horse.

> Thoroughbred horses were the product of selectively breeding Arab and Barb stallions with swift English mares in order to produce horses with significant endurance, or "bottom." Their offspring had carefully noted bloodlines back to these stallions and were initially bred principally for course racing or long races around a track. Thoroughbred horses were bred rapidly and imported to the colonies as early as 1700. While initially bred only for racing, the breed quickly found use in foxhunting, postchaise driving, and even the new service of Light Dragoons. (Stuart Lilie, expert on 18th-century equestrianism)

Horses at the run—better known as the canter—always lead with one leg. A left-lead canter gives the horse a better-balanced turn to the left. Making a hard right turn on the left lead, a counter-canter, will unbalance a horse and make the turn very hard, if not dangerous. The same principles hold for the right-lead canter. With proper training of the horse, a rider can ask for a lead change while the horse is at the canter. Horses are incredibly sensitive. While going over a jump, with the horse still in the air, a simple turn of the rider's head will cause the horse to change leads. The horse can feel the slight shift in weight and body posture caused by the rider turning his or her head. Both horse and rider are then ready to make an instant turn in the direction desired on landing.

Page 53

"I heard the bullets whistle, and, believe me, there is something charming in the sound." Here is some context for this quote from Washington, in which he recalls his presence at the opening shots of the French and Indian War:

> I fortunately escaped without any wound, for the right wing, where I stood, was exposed to and received all the enemy's fire, and it was the part where the man was killed, and the rest wounded. I heard the bullets whistle, and, believe me, there is something charming in the sound. (Letter to John Augustine Washington, Camp at Great Meadow, May 31, 1754, in Washington Papers)

—Chapter Eight—

Page 55

"Desperate Ground": "Ground on which we can only be saved from destruction by fighting without delay, is desperate ground."—Sun Tzu

"Sergeant Justus Bellamy." As I mention in the preface and Appendix One, I drew heavily on details Bellamy provided in his pension account after the war. The following excerpt from Dann offers more detail on the pension account:

Many years after the war veterans had to make a deposition to prove their war time service to get a pension. This account was taken from that record. Here is the account in his own words unedited: "Deponent [Bellamy] then remained in New York until our army was driven out by the British. On the retreat from the city, deponent was drafted into the rear to the guard the baggage and cannon. On the retreat to Harlem or Kingsbridge, we were all the way fired at by the British and cut off amazingly, and deponent expected to be killed but resolved to sell his life as dearly as possible. We made a sort of fortification of rails at Harlem Heights, a little west of the road. We soon found ourselves surrounded, and, on finding no word of command given and on looking about, there was no person in command or that ranked higher than deponent. Deponent then counted and saw that of all, there were but seventy left. He immediately took charge and said to the men that it was best to mount on top of the rails and let them fire at us and then fall back and then pounce upon them in their smoke. We did so, and when they were reloading we rushed upon them with our bayonets and cut all who went in front of us down. When we felt that we touched them with our bayonets, we pulled the trigger and fired and in this way cut them all down when we met them. Our different platoons each met them in this way as they approached, but at the same time our party kept retreating as fast as the enemy formed and came up. (Dann, pp. 387 and 388)

Page 56

"Prime and load." The musket [aka firelock, flintlock] had a small hole [touch hole] at the base of the barrel. Prime: gunpowder would be added to the pan by the touch hole. Upon pulling the trigger, the flint would strike a spark against the steel. The gunpowder would ignite in the pan, which in turn would ignite the powder in the barrel through the touch hole. The explosion would then fire the bullet out of the barrel. Load: the cartridge would be rammed down the barrel, much as it is for the cannon.

"Prison ships." The British held many Continental Army prisoners of war in old ships, which were no longer seaworthy, in New York City harbor. The ships were floating concentration camps. The prisoners were kept malnourished, given rotten food to eat and filthy water to drink, and were denied warm clothing and blankets. It's no mystery how over 11,000 men died on those prison ships. This website has more detail and the location of the memorial: (http://prisonshipmartyrs.com/monument.html).

Page 59

"Make room for the General! He is coming on fast! He is going to jump the barricade!" Here is Bellamy's account of Washington, pursued by British horse, as the General passed through Bellamy's men:

> When we had retreated as far as the woods, when we filed off and went to the road, and when we had passed a small fortification, we saw General Washington coming on [his] horse and the British cavalry after him. We opened to the right and left and let him pass. When the British horse come up, the front rank kneeled down and set their bayonets so as to strike their horses in their breast, and the rear ranks stood up and fired at the horsemen. They were cut down, and the riders were thrown from their horses, and we stopped their progress, and they returned and gave up the chase. (Dann, p. 388)

"As much as the people of this new country feared a standing army..." One of the significant reasons for the Revolution was the dislike of the concept of a standing army. Even before the war, many of the colonists saw British troops, or "Regulars," as instruments of tyranny. They were forced to quarter troops in their own homes. There had also been incidents such as the Boston Massacre.

Two views are shared below. In the first passage, Washington refers to Patrick Henry, speaking before the war:

> On March 23 Patrick Henry introduced resolutions looking to the arming of the colony. The convention resolved "that a well regulated militia, composed of gentlemen and yeomen, is the natural strength and only security of a free government; that such a militia in this colony would forever render it unnecessary for the mother country to keep among us, for the purpose of our defense, any standing army of mercenary forces, always subversive of the quiet, and dangerous to the liberties, of the people, and would obviate the pretext of taxing us for their support." (George Washington to John A. Washington, March 25, 1775, in Washington Papers)

In the second passage Washington presents an argument to Congress about the need for a permanent standing army:

> When their want of discipline and refusal, of almost every kind of restraint and Government, have produced a like conduct but too common to the whole, and an entire disregard of that order and Subordination necessary to the well doing of an Army, and which had been inculcated before, as well as the nature of our Military establishment would admit of, our Condition is still more Alarming, and with the deepest concern I am obliged to confess my want of confidence, in the generality of the Troops. All these circumstances fully confirm the Opinion I ever entertained, and which I more than once in my letters took the Liberty of mentioning to Congress, That no dependence could be in a Militia or other Troops than those enlisted and embodied for a longer period than our regulations heretofore have prescribed. I am persuaded and as fully convinced, as I am of any one fact that has happened, that

our Liberties must of necessity be greatly hazarded, If not entirely lost, if their defense is left to any but a permanent standing Army, I mean one to exist during the War. (George Washington to Continental Congress, September 2, 1776, in Washington Papers)

Page 60

"Dragoon weapons." A carbine is a musket made about 1 foot shorter than an infantry musket so that it can be handled on horseback. It is much more accurate than a pistol. A dragoon arrives at a battle mounted and can continue fighting on horseback or dismount and fight on foot. A dragoon's standard issue weapons were: a saber (curved sword), two pistols, a carbine, and a bayonet.

—Chapter Ten—

Page 63

"Lieutenant Colonel Thomas Knowlton." Knowlton commanded a unit that became known as Knowlton's Rangers, a select group that was part of Colonel John Durkee's 20th Continental Regiment from Connecticut. (For information on this regiment, go to: http://www.americanwars.org/ct-american-revolution/colonel-john-durkees-regiment-1776.htm)

Knowlton's Rangers were not "Rangers" in the strictest sense – that is, in the same sense as the famous "Rogers Rangers" of the French and Indian War, from which today's U.S. Army Rangers are considered to descend. Still, Knowlton's Rangers did perform many daring missions, and today the Military Intelligence Corps has a Knowlton Award to honor excellence in service. The Corps established the award in 1995; it is described as follows at http://www.knowlton.4t.com/knowlton7/:

> LTC Thomas Knowlton's distinguished military service during the Revolutionary War was recognized by General

George Washington, who appointed him to raise a regiment, expressly for desperate and delicate intelligence services. Knowlton exemplifies the gallantry, bravery and strong determination to succeed associated with the Military Intelligence soldier. As a brave warrior soldier, and the first intelligence professional in the Continental Army, LTC Thomas Knowlton embodies courage and dedication to duty. He is an appropriate symbol of excellence for the Military Intelligence Corps.

Page 64
"Knowlton led a detachment of 200 men.... The audience laughed uproariously thinking it was part of the play" (Harris, p. 56).

"But soon finding their mistake...women fainting, etc." (McCullough, p. 75).

"Washington had the kindest look in his eyes that Knowlton had ever seen." A character observation of Washington by Lemuel Cook, a soldier who met him in person (Cook, p. 47).

Page 65
"[W]e shall display in the extended order at 5-pace intervals." Contrary to popular thought, 18th-century soldiers did not always fight and move shoulder to shoulder. In the extended order, each man would be several paces from the next, in this case 5-paces.

"The second section will break off." The Continental Army operated with a two-rank system, with the two ranks facing the enemy. With the command "Section break off," the second rank would move to the left and line up with the first rank.

"At the rout step." This means not in step.

"**Knowlton would never say 'go on boys,'** it is always 'come on boys'" (Pension account of David Thorp of Woodbury, Connecticut, a veteran of Knowlton's Rangers, cited in Johnston, p. 195).

—Chapter Eleven—

Page 69-70
"**Lieutenant Abner Bacon**" and "**Sergeant David Thorp.**" Both men participated in the battle and fought with Knowlton (Johnston, p. 195).

Page 71
"**The 2nd and 3rd Light Infantry Battalions**" (Johnston, p. 63).

"**Highlanders**" were hardy men from the Scottish Highlands, who were very tough, hard fighting soldiers. I go into some detail here to reinforce the point that the Patriots engaged at the Battle of Harlem Heights were up against some of the finest troops in Great Britain. The following is an eyewitness account of the furious assault at the French Fort Carillon (later renamed Fort Ticonderoga by the British). The battle took place in July 1758 in what is now New York State, at the upper end of Lake George:

> The intrepid conduct of the Highlanders on this occasion was made the topic of universal panegyric in Great Britain, and the public spirits teemed with honorable testimonies to their bravery. If anything could add to the gratification they received from the approbation of their country, nothing was better calculated to enhance it than the handsome way in which their services were appreciated by their companions in arms. 'With a mixture of esteem, grief, and envy (says an officer of the 55th), I consider the great loss and immortal glory acquired by the Scots Highlanders in the late bloody affair. Impatient for orders, they rushed forward to the entrenchments, which many of them actually mounted. They

appeared like lions breaking from their chains. Their intrepidity was rather animated than damped by seeing their comrade's fall on every side. I have only to say of them, that they seemed more anxious to revenge the cause of their deceased friends, than careful to avoid the same fate. By their assistance, we expect soon to give a good account of the enemy and of ourselves. There is much harmony and friendship between us. (From Murray McCombs, "Scottish Regiments: The Black Watch – Ticonderoga," at http://www.electric scotland.com/history/scotreg/bwatch/bw6.htm

"Hessians." During the American Revolutionary War, Landgrave Frederick II of Hesse-Kassel (then a province in the German state of Hesse) and other German princes hired out some of their regular army units to Great Britain to fight against the rebels in the American Revolution. About 30,000 of these men served in North America. They were called Hessians because the largest group (12,992 of the total 30,067 men) came from Hesse-Kassel. See http://en.wikipedia.org/wiki/Hessian_(soldiers).

"Seven Years' War." Referred to as the French and Indian War in U.S. history, the Seven Years' War (1756-1763), as it is known in European history, started in the Colonies in 1754. It went on to become a world war, with fighting in Europe beginning in 1756. Ironically, many historians put the blame on George Washington for starting it. During that war, Americans were allied with their mother country England. In what is now Pittsburgh, Pennsylvania, Washington led the Virginia Regiment in firing the first shots at the French. However, tensions between France and Britain were at the breaking point. Both were in extreme competition to control the New World. Even without the incident with Washington, something would have set off the war.

Page 72
"400 men under his command" (from the eye-witness account of

Captain Stephen Brown, who served with the Rangers on that fateful day; in Johnston, p. 155).

"Let them see that we can stand and fight! Panics don't last overnight!" (Johnston, p. 61).

Page 73
"Each Ranger had fired eight rounds." The firsthand account below was most likely made by Captain Stephen Brown according to Johnston.

> After giving them eight rounds a piece the Colonel gave orders for retreating…(Johnston, p. 155)

Page 74
"Knowlton got the men in position behind the low stone wall." From an eye-witness account by Judge Oliver Burnham, Cornwall, Connecticut, one of Knowlton's Rangers (in Johnston, p. 178).

Page 75
"The British Light Troops had been keeping up what for the moment seemed to them a merry chase" (Johnston, p. 66).

"Hark! Hark! The bugle's lofty sound . . . ." From a period song sung by the British Light Infantry (Johnston, p. 67).

Page 76
"I never felt such a sensation before—it seemed to crown our disgrace." Actual quote from Joseph Reed (Johnston, p. 68).

"Men could sense this unseen power" (Chernow, p. XX).

—Chapter Twelve—

Page 78
"[T]o recover its military ardor, which is of the utmost moment to an army" (letter from George Washington to Patrick Henry, in Johnston, p. 68).

"**Weedon's 3ʳᵈ Virginia Regiment.**" Three companies from the regiment took part (Johnston, p. 75).

"**Marylanders with the Flying Camp.**" The Maryland Flying Camp was made up of troops from General Beale's Brigade—nine companies in all (Johnston, p. 82).

More on "Flying Camp:"

> When the British evacuated Boston in Mar. 76 the Americans were faced with the need for defending widely scattered areas where the enemy might strike next. Part of their solution was the establishment of a "flying camp," the term being a literal translation of *camp volant,* and in the military doctrine of the day meaning a mobile, strategic reserve. (Boatner, p. 371)

Page 79
"**Lieutenant Colonel Archibald Crary of Hitchcock's Rhode Island Regiment led 150 of his men out to the Hollow Way**" (paraphrased from Johnston, p. 69).

"**Nixon's entire Brigade, some 900 strong, took position in a heavily wooded area on the edge of the Hollow Way**" (paraphrased from Johnston, p. 70).

Page80
"**Jaeger riflemen.**" Rifled muskets were much more accurate than the smooth-bore muskets used by most soldiers at the time. However,

rifled muskets took much longer to load and could not be fitted with a bayonet. Soldiers with muskets and bayonets provided vital support when confronted with an enemy bayonet charge.

> The average Hessian Regiment was five companies of about 100 men. One of which was the Grenadier company, no light infantry company [the other four company's would be hat companies.] Grenadiers were massed into battalions similar to the British they wore tall conical helmets. The Jaegers were supported by a Hessian Grenadier Battalion, after the rebels pounded the British light Infantry at Harlem Heights The Jaegers also wore hats. Only the grenadiers had the conical helmets. It's a common misconception that all Hessian solders wore helmets. (Paraphrased from a conversation with John Lopez of the reenactment unit Landgraf von Wutginau.)

Page 81
"A junior officer in the 3rd Virginia Regiment was well ahead of the column, acting as a scout. He began directing the men to turn west, toward the Redcoats. Reed was troubled. They were heading west too soon" (paraphrased from Johnston, p. 76).

—Chapter Thirteen—

Page 83
"Wreden stepped forward 20 paces by himself to get a better shot and targeted one of the senior officers" (paraphrased from a firsthand account of the battle by a Hessian, in Johnston, p. 226).

"I do not value my life if we but get the day", in Knowlton's Ranger's Captain Stephen Brown's eyewitness account of Knowlton's last words (Johnston, p. 78).

Page 84

"By all means, keep up this flank attack." Actual quote from Captain Brown's account: "He desired me by all means to keep up this flank" (Johnston, p. 78).

"As he was carried away Brown was struck by Knowlton's demeanor. He seemed as unconcerned and calm as though nothing had happened to him" (paraphrased from Captain Brown's firsthand account of the battle, in Johnston, p. 78).

Page 85

"Communication between the Germans and British was often difficult. Wreden and Prentiss both knew French." French was the diplomatic language of the 18th century in Europe. Most Europeans from the upper class, from which officers would come, spoke French. Here is an interesting discussion on the topic:

> Bauermeister [Major Carl von Bauermeister, the Adjutant General for the Hessian Corps in America] mentions in his journal that the British frequently returned troop and equipment lists which were "not formatted to their liking." Whether or not this is an allusion to a language barrier problem cannot be determined, as Bauermeister does not elaborate further.

> Von Donop [Count Carl Emil Ulrich von Donop, colonel, commander of the prestigious Hessian Jäger Corps] frequently referred to how invaluable LTC Thomas Sterling of the 42nd was to him during the Jersey Campaign of 1776, as Thomas Sterling spoke German rather well and helped Von Donop read James Grants' communiqués. When Sterling was sent south in late December to Mt Holly, [V]on Donop mentioned in his letters to Rall how much this upset his communication with Grant (who was apparently writing in English). These letters are readily

available in the appendices of Stryker's book on the Battles of Trenton and Princeton.

Captain George Pausch of the Hanau artillery company frequently mentions language barrier issues between the Germans (Brunswickers) and the English in his diary. [H]e writes that the British are so haughty as to expect the Germans to communicate with them in English, despite the fact that all parties concerned could speak French. (British and Hessian Communication, Message Number 141684, Yahoo Group – Rev List, Timothy Logue, Historian)

Page 87

"Two Hessians stood up Baines's limp body and held him against a tree. A third man drove Baines's own bayonet through his body, pinning him to the tree." There are documented cases of this atrocity being enacted by Hessians with Continentals (McCullough, pp. 181 and 213).

Page 89

"Stroup was born in America, but his parents had emigrated from Germany." Many German immigrants fought on the side of the Continentals. The 8th Maryland Regiment (also known as the German Regiment) was one example. A military police unit named after its commander, Captain Bartholomew von Heer, performed many duties in the war, including providing security for General Washington. Each of these units was made up entirely of Germans. (See http://en.wikipedia.org/wiki/Germans_in_the_American_Revoluti on.)

Stroup is a fictitious character, but I included him in the story as a salute to the modern military and to acknowledge a friend, a fellow re-enactor, whose name is Stroup. All of his four sons are on active duty in the U.S. armed services. The birth of the U.S. Army is traced to 1775. There is an unbroken link from that year to the lineage of today's U.S. Army. In using the name Stroup, I am alluding to that connection. I also want to honor my friend. It is unusual for a father to have his entire progeny on active duty. It is a great sacrifice. I did not give my character Stroup a first name in the book because he is meant to represent the four sons. The name also fit well with the scenario because it is German. The character Stroup was able to speak German fluently to the Hessians. As stated above, many German Americans fought in the Continental Army.

—Chapter Fifteen—

Page 97
"The God of Armies." Washington seemed to go out of his way to refer to God in different ways. This was a common practice among preachers of the 18th century. The Bible has many names for God. Here is an example of where Washington used the phrase:

> ...and to bid a final adieu to the Armies he has so long had the honor to Command, he can only again offer in their behalf his recommendations to their grateful country, and his prayers to the *God of Armies*." (George Washington to Continental Army, November 2, 1783, Farewell Orders, in Washington Papers)

For a more in-depth discussion on this topic, please visit my website at www.johnkoopmaniii.com. Click "Articles," then select "George Washington and the Bible."

GENERAL ORDERS Headquarters, Harlem Heights, September 17, 1776 (Washington Papers).

Page 99
"That quote is from Proverbs."

A man that hath friends must shew himself friendly: and there is a friend that sticketh closer than a brother. (Proverbs, 18:24 KJV)

—Chapter Sixteen—

Page 102
"Those gallant and persevering men who had resolved to defend the rights of their invaded country so long as the war should continue" (George Washington, Cessation of Hostilities, April 19, 1783, in Washington Papers).

"The sacred fire of liberty" (George Washington, First Inaugural Address to Congress, April 30, 1789, in Washington Papers).

Page 102-103
"I was struck with his noble and venerable appearance. . . . The soldiers, tho' starving at times, in a manner adored him" (Hunter, pp. 76–82).

—Epilogue—

Page 105
"The Throgs Neck area was really more of an island than a peninsula, as it was shown on the map used by Howe; it connected to the mainland only at low tide" (paraphrased from McCullough, p. 229).

—Appendix One—

Page 107
Editor's Note (Dann, pp. 379–380).

Page 108
Bellamy's Account of the Battle of Danbury (Dann, pp. 389–390).

Sources

Sources are listed in alphabetical order according to the notation used in the text.

Abbott family
Abbott family website:
(http://abbottfamily.weebly.com/revolutionary-war-1775-1783.html).

Anderson
Fred Anderson, ed., *George Washington Remembers: Reflections on the French & Indian War* (Lanham, MD: Rowman & Littlefield, 2004).

Bangs letter
Edward Bangs, ed., *Isaac Bangs in His Own Words—The Journal of Lieutenant Isaac Bangs, April 1 to July 29, 1776* (Cambridge, MA: John Wilson and Son, University Press, 1890, p. 12.)

Beck
Derek W. Beck, *Journal of the American Revolution—Dissecting the Timeline of Paul Revere's Ride,* April 9, 2014: (http://allthingsliberty.com/2014/04/dissecting-the-timeline-of-paul-reveres-ride/).

Bell
J.L. Bell, *Boston 1775 – Did Gen. Washington engage in any disinformation campaigns during the siege of Boston?* (http://boston1775.blogspot.com/2011/03/unanswered-question-2.html).

Chernow
Ron Chernow, *Washington: A Life.* New York: Penguin Press, 2010.

Cook
Frank W. Cook, "Lemuel Cook Meets George Washington," *Patriots of the American Revolution 4.* January–February 2011, p. 47.

Custis
George Washington Parke Custis, *Recollections and Private Memoirs of Washington* (Washington, DC: William H. Moore, 1859). Available at: (http://leearchive.wlu.edu/washington/reference/custis/index.html).

Dann
John C. Dann, ed., *The Revolution Remembered: Eyewitness Accounts of the War for Independence.* Chicago: University of Chicago Press, 1983.

Flexner
James Thomas Flexner, *George Washington: The Forge of Experience, 1732–1775.* Boston: Little, Brown and Co., 1965.

German Americans
(http://en.wikipedia.org/wiki/Germans_in_the_American_Revol
ution).

Gordon letter
Letter from Rev. William Gordon to Samuel Wilcon, April 6,
1776. *Proceedings of the Massachusetts Historical Society*, vol. LX,
Oct. 1926–June 1927, p. 362.

Greene
Jerome A. Greene, *The Guns of Independence: the Siege of Yorktown,
1781*. New York: Savas Beatie, 2005.

Harris
John Harris, "Washington's First Victory—The Liberation of
Boston," *Boston Globe*, insert for the Nation's 200th Anniversary,
March 7, 1976.

Hayball
David M. Hayball, "George Washington's Generals: Major General
Nathanael Greene": (http://www.revolutionarywararchives.org/greene
hay.html).

Hickman
Kennedy Hickman, "American Revolution: Major General Charles
Lee": (http://militaryhistory.about.com/od/americanrevolutio1/p/
American-Revolution-Major-General-Charles-Lee.htm).

Hunter
"An Account of a Visit Made to Washington at Mount Vernon, by
an English Gentleman, in 1785," *Pennsylvania Magazine of History
and Biography* (1893), pp. 76–82. (Diary of Robert Hunter Jr., also
known as John Hunter [Most likely to differentiate him from his
father, Robert Sr.]): (https://archive.org/stream/pennsylvania
maga17histuoft#page/76/mode/2up/search/vernon).

Jackson and Twohig
Donald Jackson, ed., and Dorothy Twohig, assoc. ed., *The Diaries of George Washington,* The Papers of George Washington. Charlottesville: University Press of Virginia, 1978.

Johnston
Henry Phelps Johnston, *The Battle of Harlem Heights, September 16, 1776, with a Review of the Events of the Campaign.* New York: Published for Columbia University Press by the Macmillan Co., London, 1897.

Lillback
Peter A. Lillback with Jerry Newcombe, *George Washington's Sacred Fire.* Bryn Mawr, PA: Providence Forum Press, 2006.

McCullough
David McCullough, *1776.* New York: Simon & Schuster, 2005.

Mount Vernon Website
Article on Billy Lee: (http://www.mountvernon.org/educational-resources/for-students/meet-people-from-the-past/billy-lee/).

Muller
John Muller, *A Treatise of Artillery 1780.* Bloomfield, Ontario, Canada: Museum Restoration Service, 1977.

17th LD
17th Light Dragoons website: (http://www.17ld.blogspot.com/p/history.html).

Shulham
Molyneux Shulham, *The Despatches [sic] of Molyneux Shulham, Vice-Admiral of the Blue and Commander-in-Chief of His Britannic Majesty's Ships in North America, January–July, 1776.* New York: De Vinne Press, for the Naval History Society, 1913: (Available

at: http://www.archive.org/stream/molyneuxshuldham00shulrich#
page/20/mode/2up).

Stevens
William Stevens, *A System for the Discipline of the Artillery.* Albany,
NY: Webster's & Skinners, 1815.

Thomas letter
Letter from Gen. John Thomas to his wife, dated March 9, 1776.
From a blog posted by J. L. Bell: (http://boston1775.blogspot.com/
2010/03/john-thomas-writes-home-to-his-wife.html).

Thompson
Mary V. Thompson, Research Historian at Mount Vernon Estate
& Gardens, "Horses and Horsemanship at Mount Vernon," 2009–
2011, p. 54. Compiled by Thompson at Mount Vernon.

Washington Papers
George Washington Papers, 1741–1799, at the Library of Con
gress: (http://memory.loc.gov/ammem/gwhtml/gwhome.html).

Wright and Tinling
Louis B. Wright and Marion Tinling, eds, *Quebec to Carolina in
1785-86, Being the Travel Diary and Observations of Robert Hunter,
Jr., a Young Merchant of London.* San Marino, Calif.: Huntington
Library, 1943.

About the Author

JOHN KOOPMAN III was born and raised in the Boston area. His passion for military history began at an early age. He became involved in Revolutionary War re-enacting in 1998 and since 2006 has been portraying General Washington at reenactments in Connecticut, Massachusetts, New Jersey, New York, South Carolina, and Virginia. He has also portrayed Washington in documentaries shown at state and national parks, on television, and for national theatrical release, including the Monmouth Battlefield State Park Visitors Center film (2013), *The American Revolution* (television – for the American Heroes Channel, 2014), and *America* (in theaters, 2014). He lives in Connecticut with his wife, Elizabeth, and his horse, Abishai, whom he often rides at reenactments. He works as a technician for an alternative energy company.

Website: www.johnkoopmaniii.com

Made in the
USA
Middletown, DE